KINGSMAN

LILIZ BLACK

Kingsman

ISBN: 979-8-9988923-3-2

Author: Liliz Black,

LB Ink serves as an imprint of LB Books.

Revised on September 2025

To my supporters —

You made this possible.

Welcome to this *world*.

Playlist

"Irresistible"- Jessica Simpson

"Feeling Good" – Michael Bublé

"Blow"- Ed Sheeran, Chris Stapleton and Bruno Mars

"Gorilla"- Bruno Mars

"Lose Control"- Teddy Swins

"Sway"- Michael Bublé

CHAPTER ONE

Freya sat at the edge of their bed, knees drawn together, fingers clasped too tightly in her lap. The muted lamplight cast soft shadows across the room, but nothing could soften the tension winding through her chest.

Across the room, Lucas, her boyfriend, moved easily and relaxed. He folded shirts with methodical grace, slid his laptop into the side pocket of his travel bag, and lined up his watch and wallet in that tidy, organized way of his. He was always so put-together and perfect.

Freya watched him. Lucas always had the kind of charm that made people relax around him. Lucas moved with effortless confidence, despite his tall stature and lean, athletic build. His sandy brown hair, often styled to appear casual but calculated, was always in place. Warm brown eyes had a way of softening even his sharpest features, lending him a trustworthy, sincere aura. Almost like a trustworthy individual.

His smile could disarm tension in a room—something that had drawn Freya to him all those years ago. His style was polished but never pretentious. Slim-fit button-ups rolled at the sleeves, dark jeans paired with leather jackets, or tailored coats. He was the type of man who could transition from professional meetings to late-night dates.

He made loyalty look easy. But beneath the polished exterior, he had learned how to hide things. His confidence consistently hovered between captivating and evasive, providing just enough truth to prevent you from probing deeper.

All she experienced was a sense of dread.

For weeks, something had gnawed at the edges of her thoughts. She was unable to identify it. She had pushed it aside, telling herself she was imagining it. She convinced herself that he was simply occupied with his work. Every couple experienced these periods where their connection grew weaker.

But the distance hadn't closed.

It had grown.

And tonight—when Lucas left his phone unlocked, screen glowing like an invitation—her instincts screamed too loud to ignore. He slipped into the shower, whistling a careless tune, oblivious.

Freya's pulse thundered in her ears as she reached for the phone. Her thumb hovered over the screen.

"Don't do it," a small voice whispered.

But she already had. Her hands trembled as she scrolled.

The truth came in flashes:

Hey, I can't stop thinking about last night.

God, you drive me crazy.

Wish I was in your bed right now.

Photos. Intimate. A mixture of betrayal, secrecy, and hunger permeated the conversations.

These conversations lasted for weeks.

Maybe longer.

Freya felt the floor tilt under her.

How long has this been happening? How long has he been smiling at me while thinking about her?

Her throat closed. A sour burn climbed from her stomach to her chest. Her fingers fumbled for her phone. She snapped photos of the messages and of the evidence, preserving what she hadn't yet confronted.

The sound of the shower stopped.

Panic seized her. She placed his phone back on the nightstand and forced her breathing into something shallow and controlled.

Act normal. Don't let him see it. Lucas stepped out of the bathroom, a towel slung around his hips, water dripping from his hair. He smiled easily. He always greeted her with the same smile.

"Hey, babe. I'll be heading out soon."

Freya swallowed the bile in her throat. "Right. Good luck with your trip."

Lucas bent down and kissed her forehead. She stiffened under his lips.

"I'll miss you."

The audacity.

The sheer audacity was breathtaking.

Freya clenched her teeth and nodded while he pulled back, grabbed his suitcase, and headed for the door. Freya consistently portrayed herself as a loyal and understanding girlfriend. She refused to act like the fool she felt she was. She wanted to scream, to shove him away, and to demand answers. But he would deny it so she stayed silent. She couldn't fall apart. Not in front of him.

"I'll call you when I land," he said with a casual wave, disappearing down the hallway.

The click of the door closing unlocked her restraint—her knees buckled, and she folded to the floor as if the betrayal had struck her physically. Silent sobs broke free before she could stop them. Her hands covered her face, shaking.

Five years. She had dedicated the past five years to loyalty. Of faith. She had built a life that she believed to be real.

But now, it felt like every moment of those five years had been nothing more than a lie. Behind her back, Lucas had been slowly tearing apart the meticulously constructed façade. Every kiss, every promise he made to her, every time he said he loved her—it was all tainted now. The knowledge that he had been sharing himself with someone else had tainted everything.

The sobs slowed. Grief boiled into something sharper. Rage. It was not in her nature, but she had learned to tame.

She grabbed her phone again, fingers shaking. She tried to block his number, but her thumb trembled too much. The phone slipped from her hand.

How stupid have I been?

Her stomach twisted, a cold, hollow ache settling beneath her ribs. She wiped her face, forcing herself to breathe evenly.

She resolved not to shed any more tears. She refused to shed another tear for him. If Lucas didnt took this seriously, she shouldn't waste her tears on this. Freya sat back against the bed, head tilted to the ceiling, as if willing the hurt to drain away.

I won't let this break me. I won't let him think he destroyed me.

Before the next wave of rage and sorrow could pull her under, Freya's phone buzzed in her trembling hand.

Sofia.

Sofia has been her closest companion since her college days. Sofia is the one person who consistently knew when to check in, as if she possessed a sixth sense for Freya's storms.

"Hey, how's everything? You okay?"

Freya stared at the screen. The words blurred. Her throat tightened.

She could lie. She could pretend. Like always. However, that wasn't the case this time. Her thumbs hovered over the keyboard, hesitating.

Then she typed:

"He cheated on me."

The act of sending those four words was akin to tearing apart a deep wound. A beat.

Two.

Then the screen lit up with Sofia's reply.

"Where are you? I'm coming over."

"No arguments."

"We'll go out tonight. You need this."

Freya's lips quivered. No questions. No, why? No, how? Her friends were like that. Pure support.

Her resolve cracked.

Tears spilled over again—hotter this time, heavier. But they weren't just grief anymore. They were relieved. She barely managed to type back:

"Fine."

HHer fingers were shaking too much to say more. The doorbell rang twenty minutes later. Freya barely made it to the front door before Sofia's arms wrapped around her. That was all it took.

At the sound of Sofia's soft voice—"I've got you, Frey..."—Freya broke.

Sobs tore out of her chest as she clung to her friend, the weight of betrayal finally too much to bear alone. Sofia just held her, rocking gently, stroking her hair.

"Let it out. He's not worth one second of you holding this in."

AAnd for the first time that night, Freya allowed herself to break down emotionally. By the time Freya had wiped her tears and gathered herself, Sofia was already moving through the apartment like she owned the place.

Her sandy blonde hair was tied back in a sleek ponytail, and soft blue eyes were focused and determined as she laid a garment bag across the bed. She looked polished yet effortless—skinny black jeans paired with a silk blush blouse and ankle boots sharp enough to make a statement.

"Alright," Sofia announced, hands on her hips. "We're burning every trace of sadness from your closet. Starting now."

Freya managed a weak laugh. "That sounds extreme."

"Extreme is what you need." Sofia unzipped the garment bag, revealing a stunning black dress—form-fitting, minimalistic, and bold without trying too hard. The neckline was a soft plunge, and the back dipped low. "I pulled this today from work. New arrival. You're my model now."

Freya shook her head, smiling despite herself. "Sofia—"

"No arguments. You gave me the code red text, and this is how I respond."

Freya bit her lip, eyeing the dress. It was perfect. The dark fabric would frame her deep brown hair and hazel eyes. The dress would contour to her curves—broad hips and a full posterior—and although she lacked the dramatic cleavage that some women displayed, she recognized it would accentuate the silhouette that had consistently been her most defining feature.

"I don't know if I'm ready to—"

"To what? Look stunning? Feel like yourself again?" Sofia grabbed Freya's hands and squeezed. "Lucas doesn't get to take that from you."

Freya exhaled shakily, then nodded. "Okay."

"That's my girl." Sofia grinned. "Now, while you change, I'm calling Layla."

Freya paused. "Layla?"

"Hell yes. We're turning this into a celebration. The 'Better Off Without Him' party. Red Lounge, 9PM. I'll tell her to bring her sassiest attitude."

She had her phone out before Freya could protest.

"Layla? Red Lounge. Nine. Freya is dressing up, so please avoid wearing business casual."

A muffled voice responded on the other end—Layla agreeing immediately, of course. Sofia hung up and turned back to Freya.

"By the end of the night, you won't even remember his name."

Freya smiled softly, more genuine now. "I'm lucky to have you."

Sofia leaned in and kissed her cheek. "You're damn right."

As Freya slipped into the black dress, letting the fabric slide across her skin like armor, she glanced at herself in the mirror. This woman was in the process of rebuilding herself.

***

A few hours later, Freya found herself wrapped in the tight black dress Sofia had brought, sitting in the plush booth of a club she never thought she'd step into.

The Red Lounge.

The lighting was seductive—neon red and deep violet pulsing with every bass drop. The air hummed with music, laughter, and the electric buzz of indulgence. It wasn't their usual scene.

But tonight wasn't as usual. Tonight was about forgetting. Forgetting Lucas. She needed to put the hurt behind her. She forgot the foolishness she'd felt in trusting someone who never deserved it.

Sofia sat to her left, her sandy blonde hair sleek and shining, her blue eyes bright but watchful. She had swapped her earlier blouse for a slinky silver top that clung to her figure. She consistently maintained a polished and protective demeanor.

To her right, Layla—her long auburn hair styled in soft waves, makeup flawless as usual. She wore a crimson dress that hugged her waist, already earning the attention of half the men in the club.

"Freya, you look incredible," Layla said, squeezing her hand. "Lucas is a complete idiot. And tonight? Tonight, we remind you why."

Freya smiled weakly, her soft brown eyes rimmed in smoky eyeliner, the effect making them look deeper, darker. She swept her dark brown hair to one side, with loose curls caressing her shoulders. The dress sculpted her curves—wide hips, full ass, and though she lacked the cleavage some might flaunt, her hourglass shape didn't need it.

She didn't feel powerful yet. But she looked like it.

And sometimes, simply looking was the first step toward becoming who she wanted to be.

"I should've known," Freya muttered as they settled deeper into the booth. "The excuses, the late nights. I just—I was too in love to notice."

Sofia immediately shook her head, her voice firm. "Stop. You were a wonderful girlfriend. You trusted him. That's not something to feel guilty about."

Layla leaned in. "Exactly. He's the one who betrayed you. He's the liar. You? You were everything he didn't deserve."

Freya bit her lip, blinking fast to push back the emotions swelling in her chest.

All around them, the club pulsed with life. Dancers moved with hypnotic grace, shadows and lights playing across perfect skin. The smell of expensive perfume and spiced liquor filled the air.

Everything was alive. And Freya wanted to feel alive, too. Sofia pushed another drink into her hand. "Forget him. Tonight is about you."

"Damn right, it is," Layla added, raising her glass. Freya clinked hers against theirs. The alcohol had already warmed her blood, dulled the sharp edges of heartbreak into something softer. The icy rage was thawing. The ache is beginning to fade.

"To being free of him," Freya toasted.

They cheered, tossing back the shots.

As the next song rolled in—a sensual, slow beat—Freya leaned back in the booth, letting the rhythm roll through her body. For the first time that day, she felt a sliver of freedom.

He doesn't get to break me. He doesn't get to own this night.

Layla nudged her gently. "So… you realize half this place has been checking you out, right?"

Freya blinked. "What?"

Sofia leaned in, smirking knowingly. "Oh, don't play innocent. You've got every straight man in a ten-foot radius either subtly—or not so subtly—staring."

Freya glanced around the room.

They were right.

Two men at the bar kept stealing glances in her direction between sips of whiskey. Another leaned against a column near the edge of the dance floor, clearly debating whether to approach. A tall man in a charcoal suit caught her gaze briefly, then smiled.

Her stomach flipped. It was thrilling. It was exhilarating, yet also unsettling.

For so long, she'd only allowed herself to care about Lucas's gaze. His approval. His desire. The notion of someone else recognizing and desiring her was akin to assuming a new identity. One she wasn't sure still fit.

The thrill mingled with a pang of guilt.

Should I even feel excited? Should I want this?

Layla leaned in. "Babe. You're single. You're allowed to enjoy attention."

"Exactly," Sofia added, swirling the straw in her drink. "And you don't owe anyone an apology for looking like a goddess tonight."

Freya smiled weakly, her confidence flickering like the neon lights above. "It just feels… weird. I don't even know how to be single anymore."

"Then we'll remind you," Sofia said brightly, raising her glass.

Layla grinned. "And don't worry. If anyone gets too handsy, we know how to throw a punch."

That made Freya laugh. This time, she laughed genuinely.

As the music rolled on and the glances continued to slide in her direction, Freya let the feelings settle in her chest—the excitement, the nerves, and the ache of betrayal that still pulsed beneath it all.

I have the freedom to move forward. I'm not prepared to move forward. Despite the feeling of complexity, I have permission. I'm allowed.

***

Alcohol was working wonders on Freya's senses. Gradually, the burden of betrayal eased off her shoulders. The club's pounding music, once grating, became a welcome pulse in her veins. The chaotic energy that had overwhelmed her when they arrived now felt intoxicating. Even the flashing neon lights seemed softer, casting a seductive glow across the crowd.

The laughter between Layla and Sofia was infectious, easy, and familiar. She needed this. Every drink she took and every shared laugh chipped away at the frustration, anger, and sadness she had carried alone for far too long.

Her gaze drifted across the room. The crowd swayed to the music, a sea of bodies cloaked in shadows and light. But eventually, her eyes settled on the elevated VIP area.

The boundary was marked by a subtle rope, an invisible line that screamed "off-limits" to anyone who didn't belong. Who didn't hold importance? Who didn't carry power like a signature cologne?

Freya understood that the city's elite reserved this space for themselves. The city's elite included politicians, celebrities, and individuals with an abundance of wealth and power.

She didn't belong to this particular group. Layla, half-drunk and leaning lazily against Sofia's shoulder, giggled between her words.

"Elite of Elites," she whispered, her eyes sparkling with mischief. "And the more elite they are, the hotter they get." Freya chuckled, shaking her head. But her curiosity was piqued.

She looked back to the VIP section. The dim lighting cloaked most details, but she could make out the silhouettes of men lounging in expensive suits and women draped in designer dresses, sipping drinks that probably cost more than her rent.

Her heart beat a little faster.

For once, the idea of being on the outside didn't just sting.

It felt like a challenge.

"Let's go up there!" Freya blurted, adrenaline making her bold. She pointed toward the roped-off section without thinking.

Sofia laughed, wide-eyed. "You need an invite to get in there. And Layla just ran out of them."

The three of them burst into laughter, causing their sides to ache and their worries to dissipate.

"I can get in if I'd like to," Layla declared, the words slurring just slightly. Confidence radiated from her in waves, fueled by the cocktails and the thrill of the night. "I'll show you!"

"Layla, no—" Freya laughed, reaching out to grab her arm.

But it was already too late.

With the kind of reckless abandon only the tipsy could muster, Layla straightened her shoulders, tossed her hair over one shoulder, and strutted toward the VIP entrance. Her heels clicked against the floor like a battle drum.

Sofia followed, shaking her head in mock exasperation.

Freya's stomach tightened. This was a disastrous idea.

But another part of her—the part that wanted to forget Lucas, to forget five years of being the careful, composed girlfriend—felt a surge of adrenaline.

She almost laughed at her recklessness. What's the worst that could happen? Her heart already lay in ruins—what else could break? They might face rejection. Someone might make fun of them. It was not a major concern.

Freya swallowed down the nerves rising in her throat and hurried after them, pulse quickening with every step.

Tonight wasn't about following the rules.

As they neared the velvet rope, a pair of security staff stepped forward. Their black suits and earpieces made it clear this wasn't going to be a negotiation. They were already moving to intercept—ready to redirect the drunken, determined group back to the crowd where they belonged.

Freya's heartbeat quickened. The lead guard opened his mouth to speak. But before a word could pass his lips, a hand lifted from deep within the shadows of the VIP lounge.

He made a single, purposeful motion.

The security froze instantly. They stepped aside.

Freya's breath caught.

Her eyes followed the direction of the signal—toward the back of the exclusive section, where the light barely reached.

A man sat partially obscured by the shadows.

No words. No introductions.

But his presence alone silenced everything around him.

Dark suit. Broad shoulders. Jet-black hair. His features were sharp, perfectly chiseled in that way that made him seem carved from stone rather than flesh. His jawline was tense, his mouth a firm, unreadable line.

But it was his eyes that held her still.

Ice blue. Their intensity was unnatural.

Even across the distance, they pinned her in place. Their gaze was cold and commanding. His eyes gazed at her and asserted their claim on her.

Everything else faded. The music. The crowd. The voices of her friends echoed in the background.

Sofia grabbed her wrist suddenly.

"Freya—what are you doing?" She whispered sharply.

"You don't go over there. No one goes over there."

Freya didn't answer. She couldn't.

There was a pull in her chest. An invisible thread wrapped tight around her ribs, drawing her forward without permission.

The attraction isn't just the alcohol anymore. It was something deeper. Primal. Inevitable.

Before Sofia could stop her, Freya stepped over the boundary rope. Her friends melted away, caught up in their laughter, drawn toward the more social, less intimidating men nearby. Her absence left her standing alone, a lone figure straddling the boundary between safety and danger.

The other women in the VIP turned to watch. Their faces held a mix of confusion and fascination. Some looked curious. Others… nervous.

She could hear them whispering, "Is she crazy?"

"No one approaches him."

And now here she was—walking straight toward the lion's den, without even realizing she was the rabbit.

She stopped before him, her breath shallow. Her lips curled into a tipsy, mischievous smile.

The dim lights overhead cast subtle shadows across his sharp jawline, accentuating every dangerous angle. His suit was immaculate, likely worth more than her entire closet combined. However, it was not the wealth that piqued her interest.

It was the power. It radiated from him in waves. It was neither loud nor boastful.

Cold. Controlled. Lethal. Every inch of him warned, "I'm not safe."

However, her body disregarded all the warning signs. She looked into those glacial eyes.

And for the first time, she felt her body flare alive.

CHAPTER TWO

Alphonse Kingsman was a name that echoed through the city like a storm warning. Not only was he a billionaire, but he embodied power. The man controlled everything—buildings, businesses, and lives. To some, he was a ruthless mafia kingpin who had clawed his way to the top, leaving a trail of broken men and shattered fortunes behind him. Others viewed him as the epitome of success, deserving both respect and fear. His influence went far beyond the wealth he had accumulated; he held the future of the city in his hands. Many referred to him as the Alpha King.

If you wanted a building approved, Alphonse had to sign off. If a new business venture needed space, it was Alphonse's land. Even the mayor, supposedly the most powerful man in the city, had to seek Alphonse's approval before making any major decisions. His reach was vast, and his iron grip extended into every corner of the city, from the financial districts to the seedy underground. Those who crossed him often found themselves submerged or irreparably damaged, their fortunes snatched away like leaves in a storm.

Alphonse Kingsman evoked not only fear but also admiration. He was undeniably handsome—rugged, fit, and muscular, with a presence that commanded attention. His jet-black hair was always perfectly styled, and his piercing blue eyes, almost unnatural in their intensity, could sever a person's defenses like a blade. He always wore the finest suits, meticulously tailored, expensive, and undeniably powerful. His presence was so powerful that he didn't need to raise his voice.

No one dared defy him. No one questioned him. Either you adhered to Alphonse Kingsman's regulations, or you faced the consequences. And that price? It was steep. Everyone knew it.

He liked to settle his after-hours business at his favorite property, *The Red Lounge,* where he could watch the city he controlled from his VIP sanctuary. It was his domain, where only the elite could join him to make and break deals. The Red Lounge was an exclusive playground for the rich, and Alphonse made sure he was always at the center of it.

But tonight was different.

He sat in his usual spot; his mood was dark and brooding, while his sharp eyes scanned the room with a hint of dissatisfaction. He was in a foul mood, with something gnawing at him from the inside. The stagnation of power bothered him because everyone around him was too predictable, too obedient, and too afraid. He needed something different tonight. Something… unexpected.

His gaze roamed lazily over the club, indifferent to the usual crowd of elites and sycophants filling the VIP area. However, his attention was drawn to a group of approaching women, clearly tipsy, laughing, and stumbling through the haze of flashing lights and loud music. The staff moved swiftly to intercept the women, and their efficiency demonstrated how seriously they took Alphonse's space. No one entered his VIP area without permission.

But tonight, Alphonse made a decision.

He lifted a hand, a nuanced gesture that halted the staff's progress. Let them approach, he thought. It was a rare indulgence, but a little fun wouldn't hurt. Since Alphonse Kingsman was a man who never denied himself anything, he was naturally curious.

His eyes lingered on the group as they approached, but none of them paid him any attention. They were too busy enjoying their night, too busy in their own drunken revelry, to notice who was watching. None of them… except her.

She stood out in a way that Alphonse couldn't ignore. Curvy, with brown hair that cascaded down her back in soft waves, she wore a simple black dress—tight enough to hug her body but not overly flashy. However, it was her eyes that captivated him. Hazel, sharp and unafraid. As her gaze landed on him, she smiled—not a polite, reserved smile, but one that suggested she knew exactly what she was doing. There was no hesitation, no fear.

Her departure from her friends and her confident approach toward him piqued his interest. Women didn't approach Alphonse Kingsman unless summoned. They feared him, revered him, and tried to win his favor—but they never came to him like *this*. Bold. Casual. His piercing blue eyes scanned her, assessing and calculating, but her gaze never faltered. She walked up to him with a sense of purpose, seemingly unaware of who he was, or perhaps she simply didn't care. *Does this woman know what she's getting into?* Despite his reservations, he found himself intrigued.

Alphonse leaned back in his chair, his expression unreadable while his mind raced with thoughts. That wasn't how things usually went. People feared Alphonse, obeyed him, and avoided crossing him at any cost. But this woman—this stranger—was walking into the lion's den with a smile on her lips and no hesitation in her step.

"Well, well," Alphonse said, his voice low and gruff. "Someone's feeling brave."

She grinned; her cheeks flushed from the alcohol. "Brave or stupid? I guess we'll find out."

"Do you know who I am?" He asked, his voice low, a quiet rumble that carried the weight of authority.

Her smile widened, and she raised an eyebrow as if to challenge him. "Should I?" she teased, her tone playful but daring.

Alphonse's jaw tightened, his blue eyes narrowing. She wasn't afraid. That much was clear. And for the first time in a long time, Alphonse Kingsman felt something he hadn't felt in years: intrigue.

This woman, whoever she was, had walked into the presence of a man who could destroy her life with a snap of his fingers. But instead of trembling in fear, she was flirting with danger. Rather than shuddering in terror, she was teasing peril.

And Alphonse Kingsman liked it.

***

That voice. It sent a shiver down her spine.

Her legs weakened beneath the intensity of his gaze; the floor seemed more distant by the second. A sober Freya would've backed off, would've recognized the fire she was playing with, and wisely stepped away.

But she wasn't sober.

And something about this man—his commanding presence, his untouchable aura—made her heart race in a way that had nothing to do with alcohol and everything to do with him.

The heat rose in her cheeks as his eyes locked onto hers, cold as ice but with something far more dangerous flickering beneath the surface. His eyes were cold as ice, yet something far more dangerous flickered beneath the surface. Heat. Hunger. His presentation felt overwhelming, akin to being in the midst of a powerful storm. But instead of feeling fear, she felt exhilaration. The alcohol only sharpened that thrill, pushing her to say things sober Freya never would have dared.

"Should I?" She teased, her voice playful but edged with defiance.

The surrounding crowd seemed to hold its collective breath. She could almost feel the air thicken, as if everyone was waiting for him to snap. He likely put her in her place just as he did to anyone else foolish enough to disrespect him.

But there was no anger in his sharp, pale gaze.

No offense taken. Just curiosity.

An almost predatory amusement.

"You're not afraid of me?" He asked, leaning in slightly, narrowing his eyes as if studying her for cracks beneath her bold facade.

A laugh escaped Freya before she could stop it—soft but genuine. The alcohol had unlocked something dangerous and reckless within her.

"I don't scare easily," she said with a shrug. "And even if I did, what's the worst you can do? Kick me out? I've already had a worse day."

A slow, dangerous smile curled across his mouth.

He leaned forward, shrinking the space between them until the world seemed to contract to just this—just him and her.

"You should be afraid," he murmured. His voice was low and rough, a quiet promise laced with warning. "Most people know better than to test me."

Freya tipped back the last of her drink with a flick of her wrist and declared, "I've got nothing to lose."

Her words lingered, not as a challenge but as a statement of truth. They were raw and unvarnished.

And somehow, she knew he could sense it—the tangled mess inside her. The anger. The pain. The betrayal. The need to numb it all. His gaze swept over her with a calculating calm, taking in every detail.

She wondered what he saw.

The slight tremble in her fingers.

The thinly veiled sadness beneath her daring front.

But he didn't call her out.

Instead, he leaned back in his seat, his expression unreadable. A single hand lifted, beckoning the nearby waiter. The man hurried over with a glass of deep amber liquor.

He took it, slow and deliberate, then offered it to her without a word.

Freya hesitated only a second before reaching for it.

Their fingers brushed.

A spark.

A jolt of electricity shot through her, racing up her arm. She shivered but didn't pull away. If anything, her pulse surged in response.

"Thanks," she whispered, taking a sip to steady herself.

The drink burned down her throat, smooth but sharp. His smirk deepened. He knew exactly what effect he was having on her.

"So," he drawled, his voice dark velvet. "What is your story? What is a woman like you doing, daring to approach a man like me?"

Freya arched an eyebrow, the alcohol emboldening her further.

"You really want to hear my sob story?"

His smirk widened into something almost genuine. For the first time, there was a flicker of amusement softening his lethal edge.

"I'm not a fan of sob stories," he admitted, voice lowering. "But you... you've got my attention."

Freya leaned forward, hazel eyes gleaming with boldness.

"Maybe I'll tell you..." She let the words hang. "If you're lucky."

His gaze sharpened—approving. Hunting. She had surprised him. And he liked it.

He tilted the glass to his lips, sipping slowly while maintaining eye contact. Then, with a motion so subtle most wouldn't have noticed, he patted his thigh.

An invitation. A dare.

The gesture was so subtle yet so commanding that it conveyed meaning without a single word being spoken, but the meaning was clear. The VIP crowd had faded into background noise, and she hardly noticed the people watching her, the judgmental stares, or the barely whispered speculation. Freya's brain scrambled to process what was happening. *Wait... does he want me to sit on his lap?*

All she could feel was his eyes on her.

Her cheeks flushed a deeper shade of red, and the alcohol did nothing to suppress the sudden rush of heat she felt in her face. This was a moment of hesitation as she processed the situation. This man—by the looks of it a billionaire—was inviting her closer, daring her to take the next step.

Her heart hammered in her chest. Her mind screamed warnings. But the alcohol—the reckless desire not to feel like the betrayed woman anymore—pushed her forward.

Be bold. Be dangerous. Be someone else.

Freya glanced at him, his expression still unreadable, but those piercing blue eyes held a glint of something almost predatory. He was enjoying this game. And without giving it much thought, fearing she might lose her nerve, she moved. The platform swayed just slightly under her heels as she stepped between his knees. Her legs felt weak, and her pulse was a thrum in her throat.

She lowered herself carefully onto his lap.

His arm slid around her waist, possessive but gentle, drawing her close until their bodies aligned. Freya's breath came quicker as his hand settled on her hip—grounding her, claiming her.

For a brief moment, she pondered whether she had stepped over a boundary she couldn't reverse.

But then she looked at him.

And his gaze—intense, consuming—made her forget everything else.

"Brave," he murmured, his voice smooth as silk. "Or stupid?

CHAPTER THREE

Freya raised the glass to her lips, feeling a surge of strength and a lingering burn at the back of her throat. She winced, just slightly, but it wasn't enough to stop her from taking another sip. The alcohol had already loosened her up, but this drink was even more intense. Her limbs felt heavy and her mind a little fuzzy as she felt the warmth seeping through her.

As she sipped, Alphonse's gaze never left her. "Too powerful for you?" he said, in a humorous tone.

Despite the burn, she stopped drinking and shook her head angrily. She said, half-teasing, half-challenging, "Thank you for caring, but I can handle myself."

Her audacity obviously delighted him, as he grinned. "Independent and strong, huh?"

"Exactly right," Freya said, using him as an anchor as her free hand slid over his wide shoulder. The move was daring, and she knew it, but she was past the point of caring about propriety. His body was solid beneath her hand, every inch of him radiating strength and control. Yet, she couldn't help but test those boundaries.

Alphonse's eyes narrowed as he observed her motions with a mix of inquisitiveness and a deeper instinct. With a powerful, possessive hold, his hands moved from her waist to the bend of her glutes. She tensed for a second, but he spoke in a quiet, authoritative voice before she could say anything.

"Tell me, miss," he asked, his tone shifting to something more serious, "what do you value the most?"

It was a question he often asked those in his circle—followers, employees, and even business partners. Few had the nerve to answer him truthfully, and some didn't answer at all. But Freya, the woman perched on his lap, didn't hesitate.

"Loyalty and trust," she said, the words spilling from her without a second thought. Her expression shifted, a flash of annoyance crossing her face as she added, "Qualities my now ex-boyfriend apparently lacks."

She took another sip of her drink, the frustration evident in the way she tipped the glass back a little too eagerly. With every drink, Alphonse could sense the strain inside her, the disappointment and rage she was attempting to numb. For her, the experience was more than simply a good night out. It served as a release, a means of forgetting, and perhaps even a way of getting even.

So, this is a revenge story, he thought, amusement tugging at the corners of his mouth. She didn't know who he was—didn't know she had stumbled into the lap of a man far more dangerous than her cheating ex. Yet, here she was, bold enough to challenge him.

He chuckled, a low, almost predatory sound. "Well, I can assure you, Miss… I'm twice the man your ex is."

Freya looked up at him, her hazel eyes a little hazy from the alcohol. Alphonse might have found it annoying and made them regret it if anyone else had rolled them so dramatically. But with her, it was different. He could see that the haze of alcohol and the raw emotions she hadn't fully processed were consuming her. And rather than annoy him, it intrigued him.

Then she smiled. It wasn't a coy or seductive smile but an innocent one, almost playful, as her tongue gently traced the rim of her glass before she spoke. "Guess I'll have to stick around and find out."

Bold.

Alphonse's smirk deepened, his interest in her growing with each passing second. He leaned closer, his lips hovering near her ear as he whispered, his voice cold and husky. "Will you still stick around when you find out who I really am?"

She curved her lips into a grin, maintaining a perfect rhythm. "Let's not ruin the night with introductions. Let's just enjoy it, gentleman."

The word was a playful jab, and Alphonse couldn't help but chuckle at her nerves. She was engaging in a risky game, and he was more than ready to comply. He placed his empty glass on the table beside him and gently took hers from her hands. As she slid slightly from his lap, his grip on her tightened, keeping her in place. His hand pressed firmly against her glutes, holding her steady.

"All right," he said in a whisper, his tone shifting to one of danger and promise, "let me demonstrate to you what a real man is like."

Alphonse got to his feet quickly, lifting her with ease while keeping his grasp on her. As she automatically put her arms around his neck for support, her breath stuck in her mouth, and she let out a little shriek. Her pulse quickened as the world moved slightly.

Alphonse carried her across the room with ease, his power evident in his firm, unwavering physique. He approached a door to their right, an entry to a more private area, his steps deliberate and assured. Freya's mind was racing with a mixture of dread and excitement as her heart thumped due to the booze.

She was certain that she had entered a world that was significantly different from her initial expectations, despite her lack of knowledge about it.

The crowd in the VIP area watched with wide eyes as Alphonse Kingsman, the man everyone feared and revered, carried the woman out as if she weighed nothing whatsoever. His hand still gripped her glutes firmly, his control absolute. He demonstrated his dominance without using words. He made a strong statement with his behavior.

Freya looked up at him and tightened her hold around his neck, her heart pounding in her ears. Something deeper flickered in his eyes, but his face was still unreadable. Freya was sure she would never forget this night, regardless of what happened next.

They arrived at the door, and Alphonse used his free hand to force it open, entering the darkened room beyond. The door behind them snapped shut, shielding the VIP section from prying eyes.

***

Freya's heart was pounding, each beat thudding so loudly in her chest that it drowned out the muffled sounds of the club below.

What is this? she thought as her pulse raced. Her skin prickled with a strange mix of adrenaline and anticipation, and her mind swirled with a thousand questions, none of which she had answers to.

A blast of cool air brushed Freya's skin as the door clicked shut behind them. The truth of the situation burdened her heavily. *What am I doing?* Her instincts warned her that she was pushing herself too far beyond her comfort zone, prompting her to ask herself again.

But then, she felt the warmth of his body, his strong hands still gripping her, holding her in place. He was the one causing her head to spin, not the alcohol. The contact between them was almost intoxicating in itself, and part of her would rather not pull away.

She glanced around the room, her hazel eyes taking in everything. It was sophisticated, simple, and elegant—exactly what she thought a man like Alphonse would hide away in. The room's focal point was a king-sized bed, its plush fabric practically calling her in. To her right were large, tinted windows overlooking the club below. She could see the blur of people moving, dancing, and living their lives as if they were in a different world. From up here, she knew no one could see them. The sound of the club was a dull hum, indicating the room was soundproof. The isolation intensified her heartbeat.

Freya shifted slightly in his arms, a silent attempt to move, to regain some control, but his grip didn't falter. He carried her to the edge of the bed, and when he finally released his grip, she attempted to stand independently. But the alcohol had taken a stronger hold on her now, and her legs felt unsteady, the room swaying ever so slightly. Her purse slipped from her shoulders over to the floor.

"Scared now?" He whispered, his voice cold and smooth, a challenge in every syllable.

Freya's heart jumped, but she forced herself to gather her courage. She wasn't about to let him see her falter. She shot him a half-glare, her lips curling into a defiant smirk. "You wish," she retorted, pushing at his chest in a weak attempt to create distance. But he didn't budge. His body was solid and unmovable, and that only heightened the tension between them.

He's strong. Forceful.

"Feisty?" Alphonse's voice was low and amused, but his eyes darkened with something more intense. He was watching her closely, gauging her reaction, waiting to see if she would break. Freya, however, was not going to give up.

She moved quickly, slipping out of his hold and doing a sidestep to get some distance. She felt a glimmer of satisfaction when she saw the fleeting expression of astonishment on his face. "This is my night," she said, her voice steady despite the alcohol slurring the edges of her words. "And while you might like to be the first to start, I want to have my fair share—"

Her words faltered for a moment as a flush crept up her cheeks. She was talking too big, too bold for someone who was still reeling from the betrayal of her first and only serious relationship. Lucas. The name shot through her mind like a spark, and suddenly the weight of her inexperience felt crushing. She had only ever been with Lucas. He had been her first, the only man she'd ever been intimate with. She had never exhibited such boldness or crossed such a boundary before.

But the alcohol gave her the courage to push forward, to shove those insecurities down. She cleared her throat, forcing her words back into place. "My fair share of experiences," she finished, feeling her cheeks grow even hotter. *God, why am I blushing?*

Alphonse let out a low, rich chuckle, causing her stomach to knot up. With the most effortless, graceful movement, he sat down at the edge of the bed, his presence still dominating the room even though he wasn't standing anymore. His eyes never left hers, and with slow, deliberate movements, he loosened his tie, his fingers deftly pulling at the silk knot. Even though the gesture was informal, it possessed an undeniable sensual quality that caused Freya's pulse to twitch.

With a tone full of confidence and conceit, he questioned, "Can you handle me?" as if he already knew the answer. He appeared to be challenging her to deny his claim.

Freya's initial reaction was to retreat. Her palms became wet, her heart pounded, and she felt the pressure of the circumstance bearing down on her. She didn't know how to handle this. But she refused to give in to his dominance—not now. This was especially true considering everything she had endured.

She straightened her back, her hazel eyes narrowing slightly as she locked gazes with him. She was not going to compromise any more. She shot back, echoing his query with her challenge, "Can *you* handle me?" She felt a surge of annoyance despite her nerves and the booze, and her voice was steady.

Alphonse's blue eyes shone with approval as his smirk grew. As though he were getting ready for a performance, he leaned back a little and rested his arms loosely on his thighs. He answered, "We'll see," in a tone that was still playful but tinged with something darker and more menacing. This time, Freya's heart was racing, but it wasn't from nervousness or dread; rather, it was from the excitement of testing her limits and seeing how far she could go. She wasn't sure if the courage to maintain her position stemmed from the drink or something deeper, but she was determined not to back down.

As they stared at one another, fighting silently, the tension in the room became stronger by the moment. He was daring her, testing her, and part of her was eager to prove that she wasn't like the others. She wasn't afraid. Alphonse sat there, watching her with those intense blue eyes, Freya took a step closer, her pulse hammering in her ears. The alcohol buzzed through her system, making her feel bold and reckless but also dangerously alive.

CHAPTER FOUR

Alphonse had shared countless nights with women.

Soft bodies. Painted lips. Perfect curves.

They came to him willingly—some seduced by his wealth, others by the rumors whispered behind closed doors. Most already knew who he was: the empire he controlled, the blood on his hands, and the absolute power he carried in every room he entered.

And they treated him accordingly. Their touch was always careful and deliberate.

Tentative hands. Polished smiles.

They obeyed. They worshipped.

And yet… they never really touched him. Not really. Every encounter ended the same. Release without connection. The encounters were filled with passion but lacked intimacy. He experienced a type of joy that concluded with quietness and chilly bedding.

No matter how fevered the act, he always felt it—the hollowness. It was as if they were attempting to suffocate their loneliness with silk and perfume.

They never ventured to confront him, never strayed beyond the elusive boundary between pleasure and truth. They wanted to please him, yes—but they never truly wanted *him*. They never truly desired the man who wore the suit. The shadows lurking behind his eyes drew them in.

But this woman… was different.

She didn't know who he was. And that was his greatest advantage. Her touch was unpracticed, reckless, and alive. Not polished seduction—simply her. The alcohol had loosened her restraint but not dulled her spirit.

Her hand slid up, brushing the back of his neck, tracing the fine hairs at his nape. A shiver followed it, unbidden. Then, her fingers moved lower—skimming the front of his chest, teasing the buttons of his shirt with playful intrigue.

Not submissive. Not strategic. Just…present.

There was warmth in her skin, a softness that contradicted the sting still coiled in her heart. He could feel it—that mix of vulnerability and boldness. She trembled for a moment, then steadied herself again, refusing to appear fragile.

And in that moment, something inside Alphonse shifted.

This shift wasn't solely due to lust. Not hunger.

It's more than just lust or hunger. A pull. It's a silent ache. The sensation was akin to the initial fissure in a stone after years of strain.

He didn't want to merely use her as a way to escape the night. He wanted more—more of the recklessness, more of the fire that defied the hollowness every other woman left behind. He craved more of her caress, one that didn't seek consent yet didn't assert dominance.

With a quick, fluid motion, he pulled her closer, causing her to stumble and fall into his lap, her legs straddling him. The movement brought their faces inches apart, her breath hot and mingled with the scent of alcohol, intoxicating in its own right. Alphonse smirked, enjoying the way her eyes widened, now locked with his at eye level.

"Share of experiences?" he asked, his voice a low rumble, his lips so close to hers that their breaths mingled. He could feel her hesitation at his question and saw the flicker of doubt in her eyes. "Does that mean he was your first?"

The question hit hard. Alphonse could see the flash of vulnerability that crossed her face. Her face flushed, and he felt her shift, trying to escape the weight of his words. She wasn't ready for the intimacy of that question, and he knew it. But he wasn't the type to offer any mercy, not when he had her exactly where he wanted her.

As she tried to pull back, his hand tightened, holding her firmly in place on his lap, fingers pressing into her hips, making sure she didn't go anywhere.

Alphonse could feel the shift in the air the moment her dress rode up, bunching around her hips as she settled onto his lap. The heat from her body seeped into his, and the subtle press of her against his growing hardness only heightened the electric charge between them. He sensed the quickening of her pulse and the flicker of both fear and excitement in her eyes. Her teetering balance between caution and desire excited him in a way he hadn't anticipated.

Her gasps and the way her body trembled against him told him everything he needed to know. He caught her, unsure but unwilling to back down. That mixture of innocence and boldness intrigued him and made her different from the others. She didn't try to impress him because of who he was. She didn't know—and that made her authentic. The rawness of her reactions stirred something primal in him.

Without another thought, Alphonse leaned in, capturing her lips in a kiss that was anything but gentle. He didn't give her time to process what was happening and didn't allow for hesitation. His mouth moved against hers with a fierce hunger, his lips demanding her submission in a way that was as unrelenting as it was intoxicating. He could feel her freeze for a fraction of a second before her body instinctively responded, her hands clutching at his shoulders as if to anchor herself in the storm he had unleashed.

Her lips were soft and warm but inexperienced. He could taste the hesitation mingled with her desire, the way her body was uncertain but craving more. That innocence, that unfamiliarity, only fueled him. There was something thrilling about the fact that she wasn't entirely sure of what to do, but her boldness pushed her to try anyway. He could feel it in the way her lips parted for him, uncertain yet eager, and the way her breath mingled with his, rapid and uneven.

He deepened the kiss, controlling her, his hand tightening on her waist as he pulled her closer. She responded in kind, her body pressing harder against him, her breath hitching as she felt the solid weight of him beneath her. Alphonse could sense her mind reeling, her instincts battling with her inexperience, but that only drove him further. The harder she pressed into him, the more his desire grew, the need to consume her whole.

His free hand slid up the curve of her back, fingers gripping the fabric of her dress as his lips worked against hers. She was breathless, her chest rising and falling in quick, frantic bursts as she struggled to keep up with him. He enjoyed the way her mind seemed to slip away, allowing her body to react instinctively. It was what he wanted from her—no more overthinking, no more caution. She was responding raw and unfiltered to the intensity he brought.

And Alphonse, feeling the pulse of power coursing through him, knew that he had her exactly where he wanted her.

Alphonse could feel the slight tremble in her hands as they clung to his shoulders for balance. She clung to him for more than just physical stability; it kept her grounded in the chaos. That trembling, the uncertainty mixed with passion, only made him kiss her harder, his lips demanding more from her, as if he could pull everything she was feeling straight out of her and claim it for himself.

Alphonse pulled away slightly, his piercing blue eyes locking onto hers, watching every flicker of emotion that crossed her face. Her breath was ragged, her lips swollen from the force of their kiss, and the vulnerability in her eyes was undeniable, but so was the fire. That fire is what had caught his attention from the start, something he hadn't found in anyone else—especially not the women who knew who he was. They feared him, wanted to please him, but her... She didn't know the weight of his reputation, and it made her bold and unpredictable. Refreshing.

He could see the battle waging inside her—the uncertainty, the doubt, the excitement. He knew what she was thinking. He'd seen it in so many others: the fear of diving too deep, of stepping into territory they couldn't handle.

But there was something different about this woman. She wasn't backing down. That stubbornness intrigued him more than he would have admitted.

"Once we start," he said, his voice cold, deliberate, and laced with the edge of finality, "there's no going back."

Alphonse watched as his words settled in her mind, and her eyes met his with something unexpected—resolve. He expected hesitation, maybe even fear, but instead, he saw the shift. She wasn't going to pull away. He could feel her decision before she even spoke it, the tension in her body telling him all he needed to know.

"You won't find a better woman than me," she said, her voice quiet but filled with a confidence that almost surprised him.

A smirk tugged at the corner of his lips. He'd had his share of confident women before, but their bravado always crumbled the moment they realized who they were really dealing with. But her, though—there was something raw and unrefined in her boldness, and it made him want to push her limits and see how far she'd go before breaking.

He leaned in close, his lips brushing against her earlobe as he spoke, "Guess I have to stick around and find out."

And for the first time in a long time, he wasn't thinking about how to end it.

He wondered how to make it last.

***

Freya stirred, her body heavy with exhaustion. The soreness permeated every inch of her body, as if the events of last night had etched themselves into her muscles. A dull ache radiated through her hips, her thighs, and even her arms as she shifted slightly beneath the covers. The soreness was a sharp reminder of just how intense everything had been. She groaned softly, trying to find a more comfortable position, but her body protested with each movement.

The unmistakable scent of cigarette smoke cut through her foggy thoughts, and she waved a hand lazily in the air, mumbling, "Lucas, turn that off." But as the smell lingered and the ache in her body refused to let her settle, something felt off. The events of last night were hazy, swirling together in fragments she couldn't quite piece together. Footsteps broke through the silence, and before she could comprehend what was happening, a searing burn pierced her bicep.

Freya sat up abruptly, her hand instinctively slapping at the source of the pain. Her heart pounded as she took in the sight before her—a tall, muscular man standing naked beside the bed, cigarette still smoldering in his hand. He had pressed it against her skin, leaving a faint red mark that stung intensely.

"What the fuck?" Freya's first reaction was pure shock, her voice laced with confusion and pain. Her eyes roamed over him, her breath catching as the memories from last night came crashing back, hitting her with the force of a wave.

The man. His touch. The intense, engulfing sexual encounter left her body ravaged by pain. She recalled how many times he'd made her come, how relentless he had been, and how she'd lost herself in the heat of it all. Instinctively, she reached for the covers to shield herself, but he was quicker. With one swift motion, he yanked the sheets away, leaving her exposed. His cold, icy stare locked onto hers.

"I saw it all last night. Why the need to hide it now?" He asked with a smirk, his voice carrying the same dark edge that made her shiver the night before.

Freya's pulse quickened, a fresh wave of embarrassment flooding her senses. *Oh god, him.* His voice sent a jolt through her, the memory of his rough hands and the way he'd dominated every moment playing in her mind. She swallowed hard, trying to keep herself grounded, but the scent of him—smoke, sweat, and sex—clouded her thoughts. Her eyes darted to the clock on the wall, and panic set in.

Shit, work!

She scrambled out of bed, every movement reminding her of just how thoroughly he had used her body last night. The soreness in her thighs made it difficult to move quickly, but she forced herself to find her clothes, adrenaline pushing her past the pain.

The man placed a knee on the bed, his movements predatory as he leaned forward, as if to pull her back down. She dodged, her sore muscles protesting, but she couldn't afford to stay any longer.

"Running away?" he asked, amusement lacing his voice.

"I'm not running," she shot back, her hands fumbling to put on her bra. "While you have money, I have to work to earn mine."

Where are my panties?

Her eyes scanned the floor in search of her panties, but his voice interrupted the silence once more. "Looking for these?" He held up her panties, dangling them from his finger, a playful smirk on his face.

She reached out to grab them, but he pulled them away, crushing the delicate fabric into his fist. "Safekeeping," he said, his grin widening.

Freya stared at him, incredulous. "What a perv," she muttered, shaking her head as she pulled on her dress, still sore and stiff from the night before.

Her gaze landed on his white shirt, carelessly draped over a chair. She smirked, grabbing it and tucking it into her purse as payback. Turning to face him, she gave him a mischievous smile. "Safekeeping," she repeated with a wink, enjoying the small victory.

He chuckled, the sound low and amused, sending one last shiver down her spine as she headed for the door. Despite the soreness in her body reminding her of the intensity of the night, Freya persevered, determined not to allow him to have the final say.

***

Alphonse Kingsman stood by the floor-to-ceiling tinted windows, the early morning light filtering through just enough to outline the figures of his employees as they cleaned up the aftermath of another night at the club. His sharp blue eyes scanned the scene below with detached interest, his mind far from the men and women wiping down tables and sweeping the floor. The club always closed around 4:00 a.m., and by now, the last stragglers had been escorted out, leaving only the silent hum of vacuums and mops.

He took a slow drag from his cigarette, the red bathrobe wrapped loosely around his muscular frame. The soft fabric brushed against his skin, still warm from the night's events, as he flicked ash into a nearby tray. His mind, however, wasn't on the night behind him but on the woman who had left his bed just hours earlier.

She had intrigued him, her boldness masking the insecurities she carried. He knew there was more to her story than she had let on, and now, as he stared out into his club, he was determined to learn the details.

Behind him, the soft click of footsteps announced the arrival of one of his most trusted men. Dressed in a sharp black suit, with slicked-back hair and the kind of professional coldness Alphonse valued in his inner circle, the man stepped beside him, wordlessly handing Alphonse a phone.

"Did you find out?" Alphonse asked, his tone flat but carrying the weight of expectation.

The man nodded, his expression impassive. "Yes, sir."

Alphonse took the phone, his fingers swiping across the screen as he scrolled through the information. The details came easily, the digital trail left behind by her as plain as day. Alphonse scanned the messages, bank transactions, and everything in between. "Freya Blackwood. Pretty simple," he remarked dryly, flicking the cigarette butt into the tray with a practiced ease. "Although she said 'ex,' I don't see that here."

The man beside him sighed, his hands clasped behind his back. "He's been cheating for over six months. If she found out, it must've been recent. It's likely that she hasn't had time to react to the news yet. He left for a business trip just yesterday."

Alphonse chuckled, a dark sound that reverberated in the quiet room. He had suspected something like this—women like Freya didn't fall into his bed after a few drinks without a reason. There had been a desperation in her boldness, a need to feel something apart from betrayal. And now he knew the details of the man who had put that fire in her.

"Pathetic," Alphonse muttered, tapping the phone against his palm thoughtfully. "Cheating and running off on a business trip. Coward."

The man in the suit remained silent, waiting for further instruction. Alphonse didn't speak right away, letting the information settle. His mind worked quickly, calculating, always several steps ahead. He wasn't interested in the petty drama of others, but this—this was useful. Freya had a connection to a manipulable man who would surely return to her once he realized what he had lost.

Alphonse smirked, his blue eyes gleaming with a dangerous glint as he turned to face the man at his side. "Keep tabs on him. I want to know when he gets back."

The man nodded, his expression unreadable as he jotted down a mental note. "Understood."

Alphonse took one last look out the window, watching the cleaners below as they finished their work. It was yet another day and night filled with power, control, and indulgence. But now, with Freya and her tangled mess of a relationship in his orbit, things had just gotten a bit more intriguing.

He turned, his bathrobe swaying slightly as he walked back into the depths of the room, the phone still clutched in his hand. "Let's see how this plays out," he murmured to himself, a small, dangerous smile playing on his lips.

CHAPTER FIVE

Freya stepped into the office, the chill of the building's central air prickling against her skin. Her mind was still foggy—the haze of last night clung stubbornly despite the morning's coffee and cool breeze.

The familiar click of keyboards, muted chatter, and the low hum of printers greeted her. Rows of desks stretched before her, the Data Analytics and Transcription department already in full swing.

It should have felt routine. But nothing about today felt normal.

Sliding into her chair, Freya glanced at the time.

Right on time. But her body betrayed her.

Her skin ached in places only she knew. There was a faint pressure around her neck and collarbone, and beneath her blouse, every small movement reminded her of the marks that lay hidden.

Her fingers drifted unconsciously to her chest before she forced herself to stop.

Get it together. This is work. Focus.

A sigh escaped as she opened the bottom drawer of her desk and pulled out the canvas bag she always kept tucked away—her emergency spare clothes. She had learned this lesson during her first year, when long hours, spilled coffee, and impromptu client meetings had taught her to always be prepared.

She grabbed the bag and rose from her chair, careful not to draw attention. She passed by the cubicles quickly, but not swiftly enough to avoid the sharp, assessing glance of Johnson, her supervisor.

He stood near the glass wall of the conference room, clipboard in hand, deep in conversation with another manager. His sharp olive-green suit and dark shirt gave him the usual polished, serious edge that made half the interns nervous around him.

But his sharp blue eyes clocked her instantly.

"Rough morning?" he asked quietly as she passed.

Freya forced a small, easy smile. "Something like that."

Johnson didn't pry. He nodded once, but the small furrow in his brow said he wasn't entirely convinced. He never was.

Freya slipped inside the quiet, sterile space and locked the door. The fluorescent lights overhead felt harsher than usual. She quickly pulled off the tight black dress—the one that now felt far too intimate for daylight.

Peeling the fabric from her skin brought back a flood of memories:

She remembered the sensation of his hands. She could still hear the low rasp of his voice. His gaze pierced through her barriers.

She changed into the spare outfit—a simple loose blouse and soft slacks—breathing a quiet sigh as the pressure eased from her ribs and hips.

She moved to the sink and splashed cold water on her face, staring at her reflection.

The mirror reflected a woman she almost didn't recognize. Her dark brown hair was slightly tousled. Hazel eyes a little too wide. A blush still warmed her cheeks despite the cool water.

Then she noticed them.

The marks.

Faint impressions lingered along her neck—marks that weren't brutal but carried the quiet arrogance of ownership. Bruises shaped like fingerprints just below her breastbone where he'd held her firmly in his lap. A shiver followed it. It wasn't fear nor regret. Realization. What have I done—and why does part of me crave it again?

Last night hadn't been just a drunken mistake. It had been a choice. It was a risky decision. And she couldn't begin to untangle the consequences yet.

She straightened her blouse, adjusting the collar high enough to hide the worst of the evidence. She reapplied a bit of makeup to freshen her face, masking the exhaustion and the secrets.

The office expected composure. Professionalism. The Freya they knew.

But the woman in the mirror? She wasn't sure if she wanted to wear that version again.

As she returned to her desk, Johnson looked up from his clipboard again. His gaze swept over her—searching, curious, but professional.

"If you need to push your morning report to after lunch, say the word," he offered quietly.

Freya blinked. He was giving her an out.

But she couldn't take it. She shook her head. "I'll have it on your desk in an hour."

A slight smile curved his mouth. "That's my girl."

And as she sat down, booting up her laptop, Freya reminded herself:

Last night is over. Focus. Work.

But her skin still hummed. And a certain pair of ice-blue eyes refused to leave her mind.

***

Freya finally clocked out after a long and grueling day. Her stomach growled in protest as she stuffed her things into her bag, realizing she hadn't had time for a proper meal. The protein bars she'd stashed away were the only thing that kept her going as she finished report after report. Her phone had been off all day, and she hadn't even had a moment to turn it on until now.

As she stepped outside into the cool evening air, she turned her phone on and waited for it to power on. The screen lit up, and almost instantly, it was bombarded with notifications. The pings echoed one after another—10 missed calls from Sofia and Layla, 2 from Lucas, and 5 texts from her friends. Her thumb hovered over the messages, but before she could read anything, a call came through.

Sofia's name flashed on the screen.

Freya answered with a quick swipe. "Hey—"

"Where the fuck are you?!" Sofia's voice screeched through the speaker.

Freya winced, holding the phone slightly away from her ear. "I'm just getting off work."

"I'm on my way!" Sofia said hurriedly before hanging up.

Not long after, a sleek BMW 2 Series pulled up in front of Freya's office building. Sofia leaned out of the driver's side, looking frazzled, her blonde waves still perfectly styled despite the clear exhaustion on her face. Her work clothes, a chic retail brand uniform, were immaculate, even though the bags under her eyes betrayed a day just as long as Freya's.

"Thank God you're alive!" Sofia exclaimed as Freya climbed into the passenger seat.

Freya raised an eyebrow, settling into the seat. "Why wouldn't I be?"

Sofia responded by swatting Freya's forearm with playful but frantic hits. "Do you have any idea who you approached last night!?"

Freya laughed, raising her hands defensively. "A millionaire?"

Sofia rolled her eyes dramatically, sighing. "I'm still amazed at how you can live with your head buried in the sand." She pulled out her phone, typed furiously, and then shoved it toward Freya.

On the screen was a photo of the man from last night— the dark, powerful, and impossibly handsome figure she had spent the night with. His chiseled features and intense eyes were exactly as she remembered, dressed in a perfectly tailored dark suit. The name under the picture read Alphonse Kingsman.

So that's his name, Freya thought. She recalled how he had asked her if she knew who he was, and at the time, she hadn't had the slightest clue. That had been the truth—she genuinely didn't know.

"And?" Freya commented nonchalantly. "Another millionaire?"

Sofia groaned, exasperated. She quickly scrolled down the screen, showing Freya headline after headline—multi-million dollar transactions, massive business takeovers, and stories of his dominion over entire markets. "This man is a god around here," Sofia said, her voice filled with awe. "No one approaches Kingsman without an invitation. And no one just walks away after a night with him."

Freya stared at the screen, trying to process the magnitude of what Sofia was telling her. Did she actually sleep with one of the most dangerous and influential men in the city? Her cheeks flushed as the memories of the previous night rushed back—his hands gripping her, the heat between them, the way he dominated every moment. She shivered involuntarily.

Sofia gasped, catching the look on Freya's face. "Oh my God, you slept with him?!" She squealed, slapping the steering wheel in excitement. "Layla is going to flip out when she hears this!"

Freya fidgeted with her hands, her face turning crimson. "It was... intense."

Sofia leaned in, her eyes wide with curiosity. "How many times?"

Freya bit her lip, trying to suppress a smile. "I lost count."

That sent Sofia into another fit of squealing. Freya, still blushing, reached into her purse and pulled out a crumpled t-shirt—the one she had taken from Alphonse Kingsman. "He would not give me my panties, so I took this."

Sofia let out a laugh so loud it could've echoed down the block. "Take that, Lucas!"

Sofia quickly dialed a number on her phone, her excitement palpable. "Layla!" she practically shouted into the receiver, her eyes gleaming with mischief. "Get ready to go out because we have major gossip!"

Freya sighed, leaning back in her seat as Sofia's enthusiasm surged. She could already picture Layla's reaction when Sofia spilled the details. Dinner with those two always ended up turning into an interrogation when juicy gossip was on the table.

Sofia turned to Freya, her expression triumphant. "You realize you just turned our night into the event of the week, right?"

Freya groaned inwardly.

What have I gotten myself into?

***

Freya and her friend sat at a cozy corner table in a mid fancy restaurant. The candlelight flickered, casting a warm glow over their plates as Freya nervously sipped her wine while recounting her night with Alphonse Kingsman. Sofia and Layla, on the other hand, were completely engrossed, glowing with enthusiasm.

"Damn, Freya, you are so lucky!" Layla exclaimed, practically bouncing in her seat.

"Kingsman of all people!" Sofia chimed in, eyes wide. "This is like something out of a movie. And you didn't even know who he was!"

Layla snickered, leaning forward, "Lucas is going to flip out when he hears about this."

"Hey, he cheated first!" Sofia retorted with a roll of her eyes, clearly siding with Freya.

Freya sighed, her fingers tracing the edge of her glass. "Speaking of..." She trailed off, holding up her phone screen. The name Lucas flashed across it, his call coming in.

Sofia's eyes glinted mischievously as she grabbed the phone and placed it on the table, tapping the speaker button. "Shh!" she hushed Layla before turning a mock-serious look at Freya.

Freya winced. "Hey, babe," she answered, her voice strained.

"Hey, baby," Lucas replied, his tone oddly sweet. "I tried calling earlier, but the call didn't go through."

Freya took a deep breath, trying to steady her nerves. "I'm sorry, my phone died last night, and I forgot to charge it." It wasn't a complete lie—just a selective truth.

"What are you up to now?" he asked, his voice casual.

Freya glanced at her friends, bracing herself. "Well, I'm having dinner with the girls."

"Am I on speakerphone?" Lucas asked, suspicion creeping into his tone.

"We'll be taking care of her in the meantime," Layla interrupted, her voice dripping with annoyance.

There was a pause—an uncomfortable silence that stretched on for too long. Freya's stomach tightened. She knew how much Lucas hated Layla and her "wild lifestyle."

"Just be careful," Lucas finally said, his tone laced with tension, before saying goodbye and hanging up.

As soon as the call ended, Layla groaned dramatically, throwing her hands up in the air. "Urgh! How long are you going to keep this up, Freya? Dump him already! He's probably cheating on you as we speak!"

"It's not that—" Freya began to explain, but her phone buzzed again, interrupting her. A number she didn't recognize flashed on the screen. She glanced at her friends, confused.

Without hesitation, Layla hit the answer button and set it to speakerphone.

"Freya Blackwood," a deep, commanding voice resonated through the phone, sending shivers down Freya's spine.

Her eyes widened as she looked at her friends, who gasped, hands covering their mouths. There was no mistaking it—it was his voice. Alphonse Kingsman.

"Cat got your tongue?" His voice was icy yet playful, laced with arrogance.

"Kingsman," Freya stammered, trying to maintain control of her voice.

A low chuckle came from the other end. "So you know who I am now."

The silence that followed was deafening. Freya's heart pounded in her chest as she tried to think of a response, but words failed her.

"There is a black Cullinan SUV waiting for you outside the restaurant," Kingsman continued, his voice as smooth as ever. All three women glanced outside the restaurant window, their mouths agape. Sure enough, parked across the street was a sleek, black, expensive Rolls-Royce Cullinan Series II.

"Get in."

Freya, Layla, and Sofia stared at each other in shock, their eyes wide with disbelief. But what came out of Freya's mouth next left her friends completely stunned.

"Look, Mr. Kingsman," Freya said, her voice steady and defiant. "Just because you have enough money to throw around doesn't mean I have to do whatever you say."

Sofia and Layla looked like they were about to faint from sheer shock. Their jaws hung open, eyes glued to Freya.

Kingsman chuckled darkly, a sound that sent chills down her spine. "Still feeling brave, I see."

Freya's jaw clenched as she tried to gather her thoughts. "I have a relationship—"

However, Kingsman's icy, terrifying laugh abruptly interrupted her, halting her speech. It was a sound so chilling and dismissive it made her blood run cold.

"Oh, Miss Blackwood," Kingsman's voice purred through the speaker, dripping with arrogance and menace. "Nobody walks away from me."

Freya's fingers trembled slightly as she clutched her phone, but she was glad he couldn't see her fear. Taking a deep breath, she forced strength into her voice. "Well, Mr. Kingsman," she said, her voice steady despite the shakiness in her hands, "this is me, walking out."

With a decisive motion, she hung up the call.

The room felt like it exploded with tension. Layla let out a high-pitched squeal, eyes wide in disbelief. "Are you crazy!?"

Sofia was now visibly sweating, her hands shaking as she tried to process what had just happened. "Freya, you need to value your life! That's Alphonse Kingsman we're talking about! He's not some random guy you can just brush off!"

Freya sat back in her chair, her pulse still racing from the call. "I'm not letting him control me just because he's powerful," she said, her voice firm, though the weight of her words was beginning to sink in. She could still feel the icy tone of Kingsman's voice lingering in her ears.

Sofia leaned in, her eyes wide with fear. "Freya, you don't know what he's capable of. People don't just defy him and get away with it. He's not like Lucas. He's dangerous."

Layla nodded fervently, her voice lower now. "This isn't some stupid fling, Freya. He finds people and makes them disappear. This isn't a game."

Freya looked between her two friends, the reality of the situation hitting her harder now. But despite the fear gnawing at the back of her mind, a surge of stubbornness rose inside her. "I'm not going to let him intimidate me," she whispered, though her heart was pounding. "He doesn't own me."

Sofia sighed, rubbing her temples. "You have no idea what kind of fire you're playing with."

Layla threw her hands up in disbelief. "Well, whatever happens next, you'd better prepare yourself, because I'm betting Kingsman isn't the type to take no for an answer."

CHAPTER SIX

Freya spent long, tense days immersed in her work, attempting to ignore the recollection of her piercing blue eyes and perilous assurances.

But nothing could erase that night.

Now, Lucas stood in the doorway, suitcase in hand, his expression easy and warm. He appeared as though nothing had changed. It seemed as though the foundation of their relationship was still intact. Freya forced a smile.

"Welcome back."

Lucas leaned in, wrapping his arms around her waist in a familiar but empty embrace. The hug felt foreign now.

As he held her close, the faint trace of an unfamiliar perfume clung to his clothes. It wasn't his usual cologne. Floral.

Freya's stomach twisted. It could be *her* scent.

She was the girl he'd shared the journey with.

Her fingers curled tightly into the fabric of his coat. She wanted to push him away. She wanted to let him know that she was aware. She wanted to let him know that this charade was over.

Just say it. End it now. You don't need him anymore.

But the words wouldn't come. They never did.

Instead, she led him inside. She smiled. She announced to him that she had prepared dinner. Like a doting girlfriend.

Go through the routine. Pretend a little longer.

The meal was quiet. Lucas filled the silence with stories from his trip, his work, meetings, and the usual corporate nonsense. He spoke easily, never noticing her distant gaze or the way she hardly touched her food.

Freya nodded when appropriate. He chuckled at the appropriate moments. She confidently assumed her role.

But the entire time, her mind drifted.

She couldn't help but think of the man who had held her with such power and without hesitation. He hadn't just touched her body; he had claimed it.

Alphonse Kingsman.

The difference was suffocating.

Freya closed her eyes.

Now. Tell him now. Say it. Say you want out.

But she didn't. She sat there, heart pounding.

She was standing over the kitchen sink, washing the dishes, when Lucas's hands slid up, turning her to face him. He leaned in, kissing her softly. The kiss should have instilled a sense of safety in her. Loved. But it felt suffocating.

Too innocent. It was devoid of the hunger she had tasted in Alphonse's mouth. Her body remained still beneath his touch. She didn't reject him, but she also didn't lean in.

"Everything okay?" Lucas asked, brows drawing together slightly.

Freya forced a small, weary smile. "Just worn out. Work's been… a lot."

He nodded, brushing hair from her face. "I get it. We can talk tomorrow."

And just like that, he kissed her again. He felt as though they were still the couple he had once believed in. Like he had not betrayed her. *Like she hadn't betrayed him in return.*

When he pulled away and headed to the room for the day, Freya leaned over the counter, staring at the floor.

Why can't I say it?

She turned back to the sink; something outside the window caught her eye—a familiar black SUV parked across the street. Her blood ran cold. It was the same one from the restaurant.

Her heart pounded in her chest, and trembling slightly, she removed her apron, wiping her hands before stepping outside. The plan was to confront the driver and ask him to leave her alone. But as she approached, the back door of the SUV swung open, and there he was—Alphonse Kingsman.

His cold, piercing stare locked onto her, freezing her in place. He didn't say a word at first, just motioned toward the open car door with a gesture that was both commanding and possessive.

"Get in," he ordered, his voice as icy as his gaze.

Freya's breath seized in her throat. She opened her mouth to retort, to tell him off, but before she could get a word out, Kingsman grabbed her forearm, his grip firm as he pulled her inside the SUV. His touch sent an electrifying jolt through her body, making her weak in the knees.

"What is wrong with you!" Freya shot back, trying to straighten her clothes and regain some semblance of control. She wore a simple t-shirt and short jeans, her casual attire doing little to armor her against the intensity of the moment.

But Kingsman was unfazed. His hand snaked around her neck, pulling her so close that their breaths mingled. "If you keep up this bravado," he growled, his grip firm but not painful, "it will cost you something dangerous."

Freya's pulse raced, her heart pounding in her chest as the SUV began to move. The car's smooth acceleration only added to the weight of her fear, her body now hyper-aware of the man beside her. The air around them felt heavy, oppressive. She managed to muster up enough courage to ask, "Where are you taking me?"

Kingsman's hand released her neck, but before she could relax, his arm wrapped around her waist, pulling her across his lap in one fluid motion. Freya toppled over, her face inches from his, her body pressed against his powerful frame.

"For round two," he whispered, his voice laced with promise and arrogance.

Freya shivered, unable to deny the heat that pooled in her stomach, despite the chaos swirling around her. Her body betrayed her, responding to his touch in ways she wished she could control. She had no idea what would come next, but the pull of Alphonse Kingsman was undeniable.

***

Freya leaned back against the leather seat, frustration bubbling up as she glanced at Alphonse. "Lucas is going to notice my absence," she muttered, trying to ignore the racing of her heart and the heat rising in her body. She still hadn't figured out how to navigate this situation with Lucas, and every time she thought of confronting him, it felt like an impossible task.

Alphonse merely shrugged, his expression calm and unbothered. "It's taken care of," he said, his voice flat and without concern. Then, he glanced at her with a knowing smirk. "Besides, isn't he your ex?"

Freya clenched her jaw and looked away, her thoughts clouded with guilt and uncertainty. She couldn't muster the courage to tell Lucas it was over.

Alphonse was not one to overlook anything. His fingers grasped her chin gently but firmly, turning her face back toward him. His eyes burned with intensity as he studied her, the weight of his stare making her feel small but also igniting something deep inside her. "You can't do it, can you?" His voice was smooth and confident, as if he already knew the answer.

Freya's breath hitched as she realized how vulnerable she was. She was perched on his lap, his hand already tracing slow, deliberate circles on her thigh. His mouth hovered near her neck, his breath warm against her skin, causing shivers to run down her spine.

"I'll make you forget about him," Alphonse whispered, his lips brushing against her ear. "It'll be easier to let him go."

Freya tried to shift, to get off his lap and regain some semblance of control, but his hand tightened around her, holding her in place. She glanced toward the tinted window separating them from the driver, a flicker of panic flashing through her mind.

"They can't see," Alphonse whispered, his voice a low growl. His hand slid down her body, slipping into the waistband of her jeans. His rough fingers found her clit, and Freya gasped, her body betraying her as a wave of pleasure coursed through her.

She shuddered, her hands gripping the leather seat, trying and failing to steady herself. "Hmm," Alphonse murmured, his mouth now at her ear, nibbling on her earlobe, sending sharp sparks of sensation straight through her. "You're already wet for me."

Freya's pulse quickened, and her breath came out ragged. Her mind was screaming to stop, to push him away, but her body wasn't listening. It responded to every touch, every word he whispered.

The ride was intoxicating, every jolt of the car adding to the sensation coursing through Freya's body. She squirmed on Alphonse's lap, feeling the hard press of his arousal against her ass, each movement amplifying the growing heat between her legs. Her breath came in ragged gasps, soft moans escaping her lips as his fingers expertly worked her, bringing her closer and closer to the edge.

But just as she neared her climax, Alphonse would pull back, his touch agonizingly slow, fingers gliding around her swollen clit without giving her the release she so desperately craved. Freya whimpered, her body shivering with need, her legs trembling in frustration as he denied her the pleasure hanging just out of reach.

She could feel him enjoying the control, the smug grin on his face as he teased her. Alphonse was a man who thrived on power, and in this moment, he held every bit of it. His fingers massaged lazily around her sensitive skin, refusing to give in to her body's desperate yearning.

Freya's head fell back against his shoulder, her mouth parted in a breathless plea, but no words came. The tension inside her grew unbearable, her hips instinctively rolling against him, seeking the friction he so cruelly withheld.

Alphonse's voice was a low, rumbling whisper in her ear, "You want to come, don't you?"

Freya could barely nod, her body betraying her with every movement. Her pride conflicted with her need, yet she had become too distant to care. She yearned for a sense of release, allowing him to propel her beyond her limits.

However, Alphonse showed no urgency. His hands, slow and deliberate, continued their torturous rhythm. He chuckled softly, his voice laced with amusement as he felt her shudder against him. "I like making you wait," he murmured. "I like knowing I control every inch of your pleasure."

His grip tightened slightly around her waist, keeping her firmly in place. Every second of delay heightened her desperation, and Freya's body began to shake, yearning for the release he was purposefully denying.

His voice, low and dangerously seductive, sent shivers down her spine. "Just wait," he whispered, his breath hot against her ear. "I'll make you scream my name."

***

The car pulled up to a stop inside a sleek garage, and Freya's heart raced as she took in the sight before her. This was not the exclusive club she had anticipated after meeting Alphonse Kingsman. Instead, they had arrived at a vast, heavily guarded estate—a modern fortress of privacy and luxury tucked away from the world. The walls were high, lined with trees for added seclusion, and security guards patrolled the perimeter like silent sentinels.

The level of protection didn't surprise her. After all, millionaires valued their privacy, and Kingsman wasn't just any He was a millionaire who controlled empires. The car came to a halt, and Freya, still reeling from the ride, felt Alphonse's hand slip from her jeans, leaving her soaked and trembling from the denied release.

Before she could even register her surroundings fully, Alphonse opened the car door and, with a fluid motion, pulled her out. He lifted her effortlessly, carrying her bridal style. Freya's hands instinctively wrapped around his neck for support, her body still buzzing from the teasing torment he had subjected her to in the car.

Her breath caught in her throat as she glanced around. The garage opened into a sprawling modern kitchen, minimalist yet dripping with elegance, gleaming with stainless steel and dark marble countertops. Beyond that was a vast living room, adorned with sleek furniture and high-end décor. The atmosphere was one of luxury, yet it exuded a cold, detached air. It was a space built for privacy, not warmth.

Alphonse moved quickly, his strides long and purposeful as he carried her past the grand stairway that spiraled upward. Freya's eyes flitted nervously around the space, but her heart thudded wildly as Alphonse carried her up the stairs with an intensity that made her shiver. Each step up brought them closer to whatever he had planned for her next.

They reached a large, intricately carved door, and with a firm push, Alphonse swung it open. Freya was astounded by the room beyond. His bedroom was truly extraordinary. A king-sized bed dominated the center of the room, draped in luxurious silk sheets, the largest she had ever seen. The walls were a deep, moody gray, accentuated by the warm glow of modern lighting. Massive windows overlooked the sprawling estate below, offering a stunning view of the night sky.

Like the man who carried her, the entire space exuded power and sophistication.

Without a word, Alphonse strode over to the bed and gently laid Freya down onto the silken sheets. She felt the cool fabric against her skin as he hovered above her, his eyes dark and filled with a hunger that sent a shiver down her spine.

For a moment, Freya tried to steady her breathing, overwhelmed by the opulence surrounding her. Alphonse, his gaze never leaving hers, slowly began to unbutton his shirt, drawing her attention back to him. His movements were deliberate and commanding, and she felt herself being drawn into his world—a world where she had no control, and everything was dictated by him.

The reality of where she was—and who she was with—settled over her. This wasn't a fleeting moment of passion. Alphonse Kingsman had brought her into his private world, and it was evident that he intended for her to stay for a while.

CHAPTER SEVEN

Alphonse's shirt slipped from his broad shoulders, revealing a chiseled chest and a body carved by power and control. Freya watched, her breath catching in her throat as his hands moved to her, effortlessly undressing her with a deliberate slowness that sent waves of anticipation coursing through her already trembling body. His fingers traced her skin, leaving a trail of heat as he peeled away the last layer of fabric, leaving her vulnerable beneath him.

Without warning, he grabbed her wrists and pinned them above her head, pushing her back into the soft sheets. Freya gasped at the sudden movement, her body reacting instantly to his dominance. Alphonse's grip was firm and unyielding as he held her in place. He lay beside her, one arm keeping her arms restrained, the other hand leisurely trailing down her body, teasing every inch of her skin.

She was already wet, her body still reeling from the relentless teasing in the car, and now, under his control, her need had only grown. His fingers grazed the inside of her thigh, barely touching where she needed him most. Freya's hips arched involuntarily, seeking more, but Alphonse pulled back just enough to deny her.

"Please," she whimpered, her voice barely more than a whisper. Her pride was slipping away, lost in the sea of sensation he had trapped her in.

Alphonse only chuckled darkly, the sound vibrating through her. His grip on her wrists tightened slightly, and he pressed her closer to him, his hardness evident against her thigh. "Not yet," he murmured, his voice laced with dark amusement. "I want to hear you really beg for it."

Freya's eyes flashed with frustration, and she half-glared at him. But the defiance in her expression only seemed to fuel his twisted game. Alphonse smirked, his lips brushing against her ear as he whispered, "Can he do this to you?"

His voice was low, a seductive murmur that sent shivers down her spine. Freya knew he wasn't expecting an answer—he was toying with her, testing her, pushing her to the brink. "Can he wield so much power over you like this?" Alphonse's fingers traced her skin, teasing her relentlessly, driving her to the edge but never letting her fall over.

Her breath came in shallow gasps, her body writhing under his touch. Every time she neared the release she craved, he would pull back, leaving her trembling and desperate. She wanted to resist, to cling to whatever pride she had left, but her body was betraying her, responding to every calculated touch he offered.

His lips were now at her ear, his hot breath sending waves of need through her as he whispered, "Tell me, can he make you feel like I do?"

Lucas had never made her feel like this—never this close to breaking, never this consumed by need. But Alphonse was different. He had a power over her that Lucas never could, a control that left her helpless and aching. She hated how her body responded to him, but she couldn't deny it.

Alphonse's hand slowed its teasing, pulling back just enough to leave her groaning in frustration. Freya's eyes met his icy gaze, his cold stare searching her face for the response he already knew was coming. She could see the dark satisfaction in his expression, the way he reveled in her submission to him.

"No," she stammered, her voice trembling with need. She cursed herself in her mind, hating how easily he had broken her, but she couldn't lie—no one had ever made her feel like this.

His hand resumed, fingers trailing across her skin as he commanded, "Beg me for it."

Her body arched instinctively, reacting to the heat of his touch. With a shudder, she surrendered, her voice soft, almost a plea. "Please, Alphonse."

He smiled against her neck, lips grazing her pulse. "That's better," he whispered, fingers pressing harder now, moving faster, giving her just what she needed. Her breath quickened, and just as she felt the tension building, so close, he pulled away.

A frustrated gasp caught in her throat, but before she could protest, his hand slid down to her legs, and in one fluid motion, he was inside her. Freya gasped in surprise as her body tightened around him. She glanced up, catching the subtle shudder that rippled through Alphonse's imposing frame as he began to move. His grip firm on her hips, he lifted her slightly, positioning himself as he knelt on the bed, thrusting in a slow, deliberate rhythm.

When drunk, the sensation had been a blur, a hazy memory of pleasure. But now, sober, the intensity was overwhelming, every stroke lighting up her nerves. She tried, futilely, to suppress the growing tide of sensation, to hold on to some semblance of control. Alphonse noticed immediately. With a knowing smirk, he slammed harder, his force breaking through her resolve, wrenching a moan from her lips.

"That's better," he growled.

When her first orgasm hit, it tore through her, and she clamped down around him, eyes rolling back. She saw him falter, if only for a second, his grip on her hips tightening, his eyes fluttering shut in his moment of stolen pleasure.

Without pause, he pulled her up by the waist and flipped her onto her stomach, then he pulled her onto his chest, pinning her there with his forearm under her breast. He pushed back inside, hard, deep. His free hand found her clit, rubbing in time with his thrusts. Freya's body arched, her back pressed tight against his chest, her head buried in the crook of his neck.

The feeling was new, this angle, this control. She'd never been taken like this before, and it undid her completely. Her body trembled uncontrollably as Alphonse moved, relentless, teasing her with his hand. She couldn't hold back anymore, couldn't cling to her pride. Moans ripped from her throat, one after another, and she heard him chuckle low in approval, knowing he was breaking her.

He was winning.

"Now, scream for me."

And when her second orgasm crashed over her, she did exactly that. Her body convulsed, every nerve on fire, as his name tore from her lips in a breathless, desperate scream. "Alphonse!"

****

After her third orgasm, Freya felt Alphonse climax deep inside her, his grip on her hips tight as he pushed her forward, chest pressed into the sheets in doggy style. She was sore, every muscle trembling from exhaustion, but this time she fought to stay awake, her mind spinning in the afterglow.

She watched as Alphonse stood up, his powerful body unfolding with a fluid grace. He moved toward the small table by the window, where drinks and a box of cigarettes sat waiting. She saw him peel off the condom, dropping it in the bin beside the table, before lighting up a cigarette. The sharp smell of smoke mixed with the scent of sex was still thick in the room.

In the stillness, Freya took a moment to admire him. Alphonse had the kind of body that drew attention without effort—strong, with some scars and tattoos, broad shoulders, the lines of his muscles rippling down his back, tapering into that sharp V below his abdomen that led to his tight ass and powerful thighs. He looked like he was carved from stone, each part of him perfectly defined, the kind of man women longed to touch and lose themselves in.

But why her? She didn't consider herself an expert in bed, unlike the women who would have fawned over him. She wasn't voluptuous or perfectly sculpted like them. Sure, she had curves—her breasts were average, but her ass was round, and that always got her attention. Still, she couldn't shake the question gnawing at her.

"Why me?" she blurted out, surprising herself with the vulnerability in her voice.

Alphonse exhaled a long drag from his cigarette, turning his gaze to her. His expression remained unreadable, as calm and collected as ever. "You came to me, remember?"

She scoffed, not letting him off so easily. "You could choose better girls for this job, ones who are more experienced and know what they're doing."

Alphonse lowered his cigarette, a small smirk tugging at the corner of his lips. "Those girls are paid actors. They do what money tells them to, eagerly." He took another drag, eyes fixed on her, a lazy intensity in his stare.

"But you, Miss Blackwood... are driven by the pleasure you've been missing. That's something they can't fake."

Her cheeks flushed, a wave of heat rising to her neck. "So what does that make you, then? Charity?" Her tone was sharper than she intended, but she couldn't hide the mix of frustration and curiosity.

Alphonse's chuckle was low and intimate—like it had been coaxed from someplace deep. He took a final drag of his cigarette and crushed it out in the tray before turning back to her. Each step closed the distance like a slow, deliberate hunt.

"Not charity," he murmured, his voice velvet over steel. "Just a man who enjoys watching someone tear down the walls they didn't even realize they'd built."

Freya's breath caught.

He didn't touch her. Didn't need to.

His gaze alone was a hand on her skin—roaming, knowing, pulling apart her composure with every beat of silence between them.

His voice dipped, dark and coaxing. "Tell me something, Miss Blackwood... How long did you go pretending you didn't need more?"

Her cheeks burned. Her throat worked over a dry swallow. She wanted to throw something at him. She wanted to kiss him. Most of all, she wanted to run before he saw just how deeply his words struck.

"I have to go!" Freya blurted, scrambling off the bed. Her hands fumbled for her clothes strewn across the floor. However, as she reached for her underwear, a firm hand gripped her wrist, causing her to stop abruptly.

What the—again?!

Alphonse's maddening smirk met her as she spun around, her panties dangling from his fingers. "Seriously?" she huffed, a mix of frustration and exasperation bubbling up.

"You owe me for the shirt," he said, the smirk still plastered on his face. "It was expensive."

She glared at him. "Since when do you care about money, Mr. Kingsman?"

His laughter was rich, deep, and vibrating through the air. "César's waiting downstairs to take you back," he said, still casually holding her underwear out of reach like a prize.

He turned, tossing a glance over his shoulder. "We'll see each other soon. Don't get lost, Miss Blackwood."

By the time she reached her house, it was nearly 3 a.m. The streets were quiet, the world dim, as if frozen in time. Lucas was sound asleep when she entered, oblivious to her absence. She tiptoed to the bathroom, flicking on the light and standing in front of the mirror.

As she washed herself, she caught a glimpse of the marks Alphonse had left on her—faint bruises and red lines etched into her skin. She ran her fingers over them, her mind still replaying every moment. He was a machine, unrelenting, intoxicating.

Luckily, she hadn't done much with Lucas lately, but still... things could easily get complicated.

Pfft. He cheated, remember? she reminded herself, clenching her jaw. Every action, every reckless decision, was justified. She owed him nothing. And yet... she couldn't shake off the feeling of Alphonse's hands on her, his presence lingering even now, stirring something deep inside her.

A shiver ran down her spine.

This man will surely lead to my downfall.

***

"You did what?" Sofia practically shrieked, her eyes wide in disbelief, while Layla fanned herself dramatically, as if trying to cool down from the sheer shock.

Freya let out a sigh as she swirled her coffee, fully aware that her friends were constantly on the lookout for any hint of scandal. Meeting for lunch at the café near her office had turned into an interrogation, and there was no escaping now.

Layla leaned forward, finally recovering from her theatrical gasp, eyes gleaming with curiosity. "Okay, okay, but... how many times did you come?"

Freya felt the heat rush to her face. She lowered her voice, trying and failing to downplay it. "Three."

Layla's jaw dropped, and for a second, she seemed lost for words, staring at Freya like she'd just announced she'd won the lottery. "Three?" she repeated, her voice barely above a whisper. Then, suddenly—"Damn, I wish I could experience that!"

Sofia grinned wickedly, playfully smacking Layla on the arm. "Bet Lucas never pulled that off," she teased, her gaze flicking to Freya with an almost knowing look.

Freya laughed, her breath catching as she let the memories surface. "He's... intense. Very intense. He had me in positions I didn't even know existed—"

"Whoa, whoa, whoa! Hold that thought!" Layla threw up her hands, eyes wide in mock horror. "You can't just say that while I'm over here suffering in the drought of my sex life!"

Sofia rolled her eyes, swatting Layla again. "Please, I'm perfectly satisfied with Jacob, thank you very much. Don't lump me into your dry spell just because you can't keep a man around!"

Layla pouted, shooting Sofia a mock glare. "I'm not in a dry spell, just a... creative hiatus."

Sofia snorted. "Sure, keep telling yourself that."

Freya couldn't resist chuckling as they exchanged banter, yet the mere thought of Alphonse's hands on her skin still caused her to shiver.

Sofia narrowed her eyes, catching the distant look in Freya's eyes. "Oh no, you're not getting off that easy," she said, leaning in with a mischievous grin. "Details, Freya. I need details."

Freya took a deep breath, feeling her cheeks heat up again. "Okay, but you have to promise not to judge…"

Layla gasped, her hand over her heart in mock offense. "Honey, we thrive on scandal. No judgment here!"

Freya smiled, setting her coffee down. "Alright, fine. It wasn't just the number of times… It was the way he controlled everything. It seemed as though he anticipated my desires before I did. He didn't even let me finish when I wanted to—he kept stopping until I was practically begging."

Sofia let out a low whistle while Layla stared at Freya, slack-jawed. "Begging?" Layla repeated, her voice a whisper again. "This man sounds like a god."

Freya smirked, glancing down at her cup. "It was… different from anything I've ever experienced."

Sofia raised an eyebrow, her eyes twinkling with amusement. "So, what now? Are you going to see him again? Or was the incident just a one-time thing?"

Freya hesitated, biting her lip. "That's the thing… He doesn't seem like the type of guy you can just walk away from. I am unsure if I can walk away from him."

The table fell silent for a moment. Layla looked like she was on the verge of bursting with excitement, while Sofia gave Freya a more serious look. "Freya," she began slowly, "are you sure you know what you're getting into with this person? He sounds like a lot more than just a fling."

Freya nodded, her stomach twisting. "I know. That's what scares me."

Sofia leaned back, a slight frown creasing her brow as she studied Freya. "Look, I get it. The excitement, the intensity—it's thrilling. But guys like him? They pose a threat in numerous ways."

Layla, still starry-eyed, waved a dismissive hand. "Come on, Sofia, let her enjoy it! Indeed, who wouldn't desire a man adept at manipulating all the appropriate emotions? She turned to Freya with a grin. "And if you're getting that kind of attention, you deserve it. I say, "Ride that wave while you can.""

Freya laughed softly, appreciating Layla's enthusiasm but unable to shake Sofia's warning. She glanced out the window, watching the busy streets, her mind racing with thoughts of Alphonse. His intensity, his power... It thrilled her and terrified her all at once.

"I hear you, both of you," Freya said finally, turning back to them. "I just need to figure out where I stand. This situation with Alphonse is unlike any relationship I've ever experienced before.

Sofia softened and reached across the table to place her hand over Freya's. "Just promise me you'll be careful. We're not discussing Lucas here—this individual has the potential to completely upend your world."

Freya nodded, feeling the weight of her friend's concern. "I know, and I will. I'll keep my guard up." But even as she said the words, a part of her wasn't sure she could. Alphonse had already broken through her defenses once.

Layla sighed dreamily, snapping Freya out of her thoughts. "God, I just love that we live in a world where you get to have these kinds of adventures. While some of us wait for Prince Charming, others are enthralled with Alphonse Kingsman."

Freya chuckled, feeling some of the tension ease. "Yeah, well, let's just say it's not exactly a fairy tale."

Sofia shook her head, but a small smile played on her lips. "No, it's not. But it's your story, Freya, and we'll be here to listen to every scandalous detail."

Freya smiled back, grateful for her friends' support. No matter how intense or complicated things got, at least she knew she could count on Sofia and Layla to keep her grounded.

CHAPTER EIGHT

An entire week has passed.

There had been no communication from Alphonse Kingsman. No calls. No message left. Not even the slightest whisper.

Freya sat curled on the couch, remote in hand, flipping through the channels with numb fingers. The TV flickered with headlines and mindless entertainment, but nothing held her attention. Her phone sat beside her, screen dark—but always close. Her phone was always within her reach.

She tried to convince herself it didn't matter. She tried to convince herself that everything had worked out for the best. It had only been a night, she told herself. It was an inconsiderate and careless oversight. She used it as an opportunity to express her anger towards Lucas.

That's all it was. It was merely a brief flirtation. Just sex.

She'd repeated it so many times it was starting to sound like a curse. But no matter how often she said it, her body didn't believe it. Her mind didn't believe it.

Her heart was certainly not convinced.

And worst of all—he wasn't even thinking about her.

She found herself scrolling again—fingers hovering over her browser. Before she could stop herself, she typed his name into the search bar. Her stomach twisted as headlines surfaced. Business deals. Public appearances. During an interview, rumors circulated that he was supporting a politician.

Nothing personal. There was no indication that he had even remembered her presence.

Is this how he plays the game? Make them want it. Make them wait. Make them beg.

Her jaw clenched, fingers curling into fists in her lap. She hated how much she thought about him. She hated that she cared. But what frustrated her even more…

She couldn't believe she hadn't spoken to Lucas yet.

He was still here. He was still making his way home. Still smiling. He continued to act as if everything was normal. And she—she still kissed him goodnight, still made dinner, and still answered his calls with a soft voice and hollow words.

She had proof. She had seen it—those messages. The photos. The lies.

And yet… The words stayed stuck in her throat.

Why can't I just say it?

Why can't I just tell him that I know the truth?

He gazed at her as if she were the same woman he'd met five years ago. He would give her a gentle kiss. His eyes continue to radiate affection. A part of her still recalled the man who had once defended her and loved her—before he gave up trying.

But every day she didn't speak, the resentment grew.

She was lying to him now too. Worse, she was lying to herself. And still, the silence from Alphonse thundered louder than anything else in her life.

She picked up her phone again, with her thumb hovering over the contacts list. She didn't save his number. She remembered it anyway.

No. Don't be that girl.

Don't reach out. Don't chase.

She threw the phone facedown on the couch and stood abruptly, pacing across the room. The air felt too still, her body too wired. She needed to scream. Or run. Or cry.

But instead, she poured herself a glass of wine and stared out the window into the night.

You don't control me. Alphonse Kingsman.

And Lucas… I've had enough of pretending.

But even as she repeated those words, her chest ached with the weight of everything she hadn't said.

And the space between the two men felt more like a battlefield than a choice.

When Monday rolled around, the familiar tension of a new workweek should've been a welcome distraction. However, as soon as she reached the office, she sensed a disturbance. Johnson, her boss, was pacing around the office, muttering complaints to himself.

"The desks—how many times do I have to tell them? They need to be more organized!" he muttered as he passed Freya's cubicle. "And the walls! What's with these walls? Is it too much to ask for something inviting around here?" He ran a hand through his thinning hair, clearly on edge.

Freya sighed, sitting up straighter at her desk. She'd seen this before. Johnson only acted like this when something major was happening. And as a senior in the department, she knew exactly what that meant—a new, high-profile client was coming.

She glanced at the other employees, all equally tense as Johnson stalked past their desks, barking at them to resolve this problem or that. Her fingers flew over her keyboard as she began adjusting her schedule for the day, knowing her workload was about to increase tenfold.

"Freya," Johnson called, finally stopping in front of her desk. His eyes darted nervously around the office. "We've got a big one coming in—huge, actually. I need you on top of this."

Freya gave a small nod, already preparing herself for the inevitable late nights and extra reports. "Who is the client?" she asked, although she could already guess what type of client would cause this much commotion.

Johnson looked around before leaning in, lowering his voice. "You'll find out soon enough. But let's just say... this one could change the future of our firm."

Freya frowned. Johnson had always been dramatic, but the way he said it made her uneasy. She opened her mouth to ask more, but Johnson quickly excused himself and marched off, barking more orders at the other employees.

As the morning dragged on, Freya tried to stay focused on her work, but her mind kept drifting back to Kingsman. Why hadn't he reached out? Could he have truly ended things with her, or is this part of a strategic maneuver?

Her phone buzzed, snapping her out of her thoughts. She reached for it, half hoping it was a message from Alphonse. Her stomach dropped when she saw the notification from her boss.

Reminder: Meeting with Johnson and a potential new client at 3:00 p.m.

As she clicked on the calendar event, the name in the description brought her heart to a halt.

Client: Kingsman Enterprises.

Freya's heartbeat quickened. Alphonse Kingsman was their new client? She couldn't believe it. Of all the companies, of all the places, why here? Her mind raced as she tried to process the news. She was about to face him again, and this time, she had to be professional and collected.

But even as she told herself that, the thought of seeing him again made her stomach twist in anticipation. Stay strong, she reminded herself, taking a deep breath. He doesn't control you. But deep down, she couldn't ignore the feeling that, in some way, he already did.

***

Freya sat in the conference room, her arms crossed lightly in front of her as she watched Johnson pace the room, emphasizing the critical nature of this client for the company. Elihaj, trained under her guidance and now working alongside her due to her experience, sat to her right. Elihaj leaned slightly forward, flipping through his notes. Elijah was more reserved and cerebral. His brown eyes and neatly combed dark hair complemented his reserved and cerebral nature. His pressed shirt and clean-cut style matched the thoughtful air he carried, the quiet observer in every high-level conversation.

Beside him sat Natasha, legs crossed, pen between her fingers as she toyed with it against her glossy lips. She had that kind of presence, built to distract. Her hair was a cascade of glossy black waves, and her curves poured into a silk blouse and pencil skirt that clung like a second skin. She looked like the type of woman who turned heads in office corridors and knew it—sultry, sharp, and not afraid to play it.

Natasha, whose expertise rivaled Freya's, was ranked just below her—a fact that clearly irked Natasha. Despite Freya's attempts to build a rapport with her, Natasha always kept her distance, the tension between them lingering just below the surface.

At the head of the long, sleek conference table sat Roddrick Freeman, the CEO of the firm and the polished face of its public reputation. He was in his early fifties, tall with smooth dark skin and salt-and-pepper hair that made him look every bit the seasoned executive. Freeman had the kind of smile that could disarm a boardroom and charm a televised panel with equal ease—a man built for spotlights and press conferences. His voice, when calm, carried a smooth baritone warmth that put people at ease.

However, this morning, he appeared strained in his public persona. His usual effortless poise was undercut by the tight set of his jaw and the subtle drumming of his fingers on the table's glass surface. The man who could win investors with a handshake looked like he was calculating every breath.

"Are you sure we're ready for this?" Freeman asked, his voice lower than usual, tinged with unease. "We can't afford to let this man down."

Beside him, Marvin Johnson adjusted the cuffs of his tailored jacket with methodical precision. If Freeman was the company's expert, Johnson was the sharpshooter—direct, meticulous, and far less focused on public appearances.

He cast a measured glance toward Freya, standing a few chairs down, reviewing the final dossier in her hands.

"We've got our best senior here," Johnson said, his tone cool but confident. "If anyone can handle this client, it's them."

Freya dipped her head slightly, addressing the CEO with quiet assurance. "Yes, sir."

Freeman smoothed his tie and exhaled slowly. "They say he doesn't do second chances."

Johnson offered a faint smile. "Then we won't need one."

Just as the weight of anticipation started to settle again, the elevator dinged in the hallway outside.

Freya closed the folder with a soft snap and straightened her posture. Showtime.

Alphonse Kingsman, dressed in a dark blue tailored suit that fit him perfectly, strode in, every inch of him radiating control and dominance. As he walked, adjusting his sleeves with calculated ease, two individuals followed closely behind him, their presence adding to the aura of authority he carried.

Freya felt her breath tighten in her throat. She hadn't seen him since last week, when he had almost broken her. The memory lingered, both thrilling and unsettling. As Alphonse entered the conference room, Roddrick immediately stood, extending his hand in greeting.

Alphonse nodded in acknowledgment, his movements precise, greeting both Roddrick and Johnson with a nod. But then, his gaze landed on Freya, and her entire body tensed. A cold shiver ran down her spine as his icy blue eyes took her in, assessing, lingering in a way that made her feel exposed.

Johnson, eager to facilitate introductions, spoke up hurriedly. "This is Freya Blackwood, our senior analyst. She'll be leading the team. Elihaj Stall and Natasha Modow will be assisting with the case alongside her, Mr. Kingsman."

Alphonse's gaze didn't waver from Freya as he walked to one of the chairs at the table just beside her, pulling it out with a smooth, deliberate motion. "Do sit," he said, his voice deep and commanding, the simple instruction carrying an unspoken weight.

Freya's pulse quickened as she nodded, trying to maintain her composure. The familiar, alluring scent of pine that clung to him filled her senses as she sat down. He followed suit, settling into the chair beside her, while Elihaj and Natasha took their seats next to her. Roddrick and Johnson sat opposite, and the two individuals who had accompanied Alphonse remained standing by the door, silent and watchful.

Freya focused on the conversation, answering questions and nodding at the appropriate moments, but the tension in her body refused to ease. Halfway through the meeting, just as the discussion turned to specifics, she felt something graze her thigh. Her body stiffened, and she glanced down discreetly, her heart thudding in her chest.

It was Alphonse's hand.

Her pencil skirt, snug around her hips and ending just above her thigh, offered little protection as his fingers inched further up her leg, beneath the fabric. Panic and heat flooded her, but when she looked up, Alphonse appeared completely unfazed, his expression focused on the discussion, as if nothing was out of the ordinary. He was fully engaged in the conversation, speaking in measured, controlled tones, yet his hand continued its slow, deliberate ascent.

Freya struggled to keep her composure as her breath caught in her throat. She forced herself to nod along as Johnson and Roddrick spoke, her voice steady despite the turmoil brewing inside her. But the touch—his touch—was relentless, his fingers moving higher, now resting at the upper part of her thigh, hidden beneath her skirt.

She swallowed hard, feeling the heat rising to her cheeks, unsure whether it was from anger or embarrassment. The sensation of his hand against her skin was maddening, and despite her best efforts to keep her mind on the conversation, the room around her seemed to blur. All she could focus on was him—on his hand and the cold, unyielding power behind the subtle gesture.

Freya shifted slightly, trying to put some distance between them, but Alphonse's grip tightened, holding her in place. His gaze never strayed from the others in the room, his voice unwavering as he proceeded with the case details, sending a clear message to Freya: he held control over both the situation and her.

As the meeting progressed, Freya's thoughts raced. She had to remain professional and keep her focus, despite the unsettling sensation crawling up her skin. But Alphonse was making it impossible. He was testing her, daring her to react, all while maintaining an air of perfect composure.

And through it all, that icy, piercing stare of his was never far, watching her, even when his eyes seemed locked elsewhere.

CHAPTER NINE

As his keen eyes inspected the open papers neatly arranged on the desk, Alphonse stated in a calm and controlled voice, "Thank you, Mr. Freeman, for assigning your best senior analyst to this assignment."

"It looks like Miss Blackwood is capable of handling the assignment," he added, carefully turning a page. "I require minimal personnel involved in this matter. Discretion is critical."

Johnson shifted slightly in his seat, clearing his throat. "Mr. Kingsman, with all due respect, Freya is exceptional at what she does—but this project is extensive. One person may not be able to manage the full scope with the diligence your company expects."

Alphonse didn't lift his gaze. "I will determine what is best for my cause, Mr. Johnson."

There was a tense pause.

"Of course," Johnson replied quickly, his discomfort evident.

Alphonse finally looked up, those ice-blue eyes settling on both men with quiet intensity. "I trust that won't be an issue."

Freeman nodded, his posture stiffening. "No, sir. Not at all. Miss Blackwood is more than capable. She'll have our full support."

Alphonse gave a single nod, then closed the folder in front of him.

"I'd like to speak with Miss Blackwood now," he said, his tone calm yet unmistakably commanding. "We need to finalize the schedule for the reports and performance analysis."

Freya was jolted from her daze—her mind had been completely wrapped in the sensation of his hand still resting on her thigh, sending jolts of electricity up her spine. She struggled to keep her face neutral, but the room was clearing out before she could even gather her thoughts. Roddrick, Johnson, Elihaj, and Natasha all rose from their seats, exchanging brief goodbyes as they headed toward the door.

Freya's heart raced. She knew exactly what was about to happen. The way Alphonse's gaze lingered on her, the way even his two accompanying men exited the room without a word—all of it told her that he was in complete control of the situation.

The door clicked shut behind them, sealing them off from the rest of the office. Freya's breath hitched audibly, the small sound echoing in the suddenly quiet room. She couldn't ignore the way her pulse quickened as Alphonse's fingers brushed lightly over the fabric of her underwear—deliberate, slow, as though testing her.

In one fluid motion, as though he were merely conducting everyday business, he reached into his jacket pocket with his free hand and pulled out his phone. His other hand never left her thigh, his fingers still pressing into the softness of her skin beneath the fabric of her skirt. His cold blue eyes never showed the seriousness of the situation as he flipped through his phone with the same casualness as previously.

Freya blinked, momentarily confused, as a quick ping caught her attention. There was a message on her phone, resting on the table before her. She hesitated, confused, before reaching out and unlocking her phone with trembling fingers.

The message was from him.

"I sent the schedule I've prepared for you."

Her mind scrambled to catch up, her emotions whiplashing from the physical intensity of his touch to the stark professionalism of his message. *What?* Her eyes flickered back to him, incredulous. He had sent her a schedule—a business schedule—while his hand was under her skirt.

"The schedule will be approved by Mr. Johnson," Alphonse said, his tone smooth and measured, as if he were discussing nothing more than quarterly projections. He set his phone down on the table. His fingers, meanwhile, remained firmly in place on her skin, his thumb tracing an infuriatingly slow circle near the hem of her underwear. "Any complaints?"

Freya's mind was in overdrive. How could he maintain such composure, such complete control over the situation, while her entire world seemed to be in turmoil? She was a senior analyst, respected and professional, yet here she was—her body betraying her, her senses overwhelmed by his calculated, deliberate touch.

Freya's breath was shallow, her mind spinning. Her gaze darted between the schedule on her phone and the man sitting next to her—Alphonse Kingsman, the same man whose fingers were now inching dangerously close to places they had no business being during a professional meeting. However, his voice, his posture, and every aspect of him exuded composure, as if he could precisely compartmentalize every aspect of this moment.

She wanted to express her protest, but the words froze in her throat. Instead, she forced herself to glance down at the message she received on her phone while she was scanning the list of meetings and report deadlines that he had outlined for her.

On the screen, everything appeared ordinary, yet the context, coupled with the lingering sensation of his touch on her skin, transformed it into something extraordinary.

"I…" she began, her voice catching in her throat. "No. No complaints."

Alphonse's mouth lifted in the faintest of smirks, as though he had expected her compliance but still found it pleasing. His hand, which had remained so still and calculating, gave her thigh a small, deliberate squeeze, sending a ripple of sensation up her spine. He knew exactly what he was doing—every touch, every glance was carefully orchestrated.

Just as effortlessly as he had initiated the contact, he withdrew his hand and leaned back in his chair, giving the impression that nothing unusual had happened. "Good," he said smoothly as he adjusted his cuffs, straightening his suit as he stood.

Freya watched him, still caught in the aftermath of everything that had just transpired. He didn't need to say anything more. His actions had conveyed a powerful message. Her skin still buzzed where his fingers had touched her, and her mind was racing, but on the surface, she forced herself to appear calm. Collected. And as he moved toward the door, every step controlled and deliberate, she knew that he was the one setting the terms—not just of the meetings, but of whatever twisted dynamic had formed between them.

"I'll expect you to follow through with the schedule, Miss Blackwood. Starting Wednesday." Alphonse said, his voice steady and composed, as though the entire interaction had been nothing more than a standard business meeting.

Freya nodded, unable to trust herself to speak. She opened her mouth to speak, but nothing came out. Her heart was still pounding, her body still reeling from the force of his contact.

Alphonse reached for the door, opening it with the same fluid grace he exhibited in every movement. But before he left, he glanced back over his shoulder, his blue eyes meeting hers with that same predatory gaze that had unsettled her from the start.

"Do let me know if there's anything else you need," he added, his tone laced with something darker, something more dangerous.

He left without saying another word, the door shutting quietly behind him.

Freya sat in startled stillness, breathing irregularly as the encounter's weight descended upon her. As if nothing else had happened, she looked down at her phone once again, the timetable appearing naively on the screen. But the room still felt thick with his presence, his touch lingering like a ghost on her skin.

She knew, deep down, *this* was just the beginning. Regardless of the nature of their relationship, it was far from over. Despite feeling confused and uneasy, a part of her still wanted the relationship to continue.

***

Freya arrived at her house, the weight of the day settling into her shoulders as she closed the door behind her. The familiar sounds of the PlayStation hummed from the living room, and she smiled faintly, shaking off the tension that had been building up since the meeting with Alphonse. She could hear the rapid clicks. The sound of buttons was followed by Lucas's frustrated grunt when something in the game didn't go his way.

Kicking off her heels, she walked into the living room and found Lucas on the couch, a controller in his hand, fully engrossed in whatever game he was playing. His eyes darted to the screen, his brow furrowed in concentration. He didn't notice her right away, too focused on his game, but as soon as she entered the room, he paused the game and looked up with a bright smile.

"Hey, babe," Lucas said, setting the controller aside as he leaned back on the couch. "How was work?"

Freya sank into the armchair across from him, grateful to be off her feet. She ran a hand through her hair, her mind lingering on the events of the day. She remembered Alphonse's touch, his words, and his command over the room. It was all still too fresh in her mind.

"It was... exhausting," Freya replied with a small sigh. "Today's meeting was enormous. I will be working with a prospective client on a new case. This new case holds immense significance. I will most likely have to work later than normal because of it."

Lucas's smile widened as pride filled his face. "That's fantastic, Freya! I have no doubt that you will succeed."

He got up and walked across the room to her, grabbing her by the arms. She gave him permission to put his arms around her, but as soon as his lips touched hers, she felt uneasy. The feel of his touch was off. His touch was so different from the way Alphonse had touched her before. The familiarity and warmth that had once reassured her now seemed far away, almost empty.

As Lucas leaned in, pressing his kiss deeper, Freya's mind betrayed her. She recalled the texts she had seen weeks ago.

The texts from the other woman. The messages were filled with flirtation, intimacy, and secrets she hadn't been a part of. It had created a crack in her trust, one that hadn't fully healed. And now, as Lucas tried to reignite something between them, it felt forced.

Worse still, her mind compared it—his touch, his kiss, everything—to Alphonse. Her heart sank at the stark contrast between Lucas's soft, familiar embrace and Alphonse's cold, calculated touch. It wasn't fair to compare, she knew that, but she couldn't stop it.

Freya gently pushed Lucas away, breaking the kiss. "I'm sorry," she murmured, her voice soft but firm. "I'm just really tired. Today was overwhelming, and I really need to get some rest."

Lucas frowned slightly, his hands still resting on her arms as he searched her face for an explanation. "Are you okay? You've seemed a little… distant lately."

She nodded quickly, almost too swiftly, while forcing a smile that didn't quite reach her eyes. "Yeah, I'm fine. It's just the stress from work. This new case holds significant importance, and I must perform optimally for it. I'm just worn out, Lucas."

He studied her for a moment, clearly wanting to say more, but instead, he stepped back and sighed. "Okay, I get it. You've got a lot going on." He gave her a small, reassuring smile. "Get some rest, alright? I'm really proud of you. I know you'll do great."

Freya's heart squeezed painfully in her chest. Lucas was being sweet, as always, supportive, and kind. But that only made her feel worse, the guilt gnawing at her for the distance that had grown between them. She wasn't sure when it started, but something had changed—maybe the messages or work stress.

"Thanks," she whispered, standing up and heading toward the bedroom. "I'll see you in the morning."

Lucas nodded, watching her go as she disappeared down the hallway.

Freya let out a tremulous breath and leaned against the bedroom door for a second before shutting it behind her. She was torn between the love and loyalty she had once felt for Lucas and the unsettling attraction she felt for Alphonse. She just needed to sleep tonight. Perhaps things would feel clearer in the morning.

CHAPTER TEN

When Wednesday finally came, Freya was standing in front of Kingsman Enterprises' imposing building. One of the emails sent out early in the morning said, "Freya was to work exclusively for Kingsman alone."

The structure was a marvel of modern design, its glass panels reflecting the skyline of the city and reaching skyward as if it were trying to touch the clouds. It was a symbol of wealth and power, and it was undoubtedly imposing, elegant, and beautiful. Freya felt insignificant in comparison to the building's grandeur and majesty, her image barely discernible through the massive glass doors.

Around her, people in elegant clothing and well-tailored suits were entering and exiting the building with assurance and purpose. Wearing a black blazer, white shirt, and a basic pencil skirt, Freya felt as though she didn't belong with them. Despite her efforts to look elegant, her modest outfit left her feeling underdressed in comparison to the high-end fashion surrounding her. In an attempt to prepare for what was to come, she tightened the strap of her bag over her shoulder and held her binder to her chest.

She took a deep breath and stepped through the glass doors into the marble-floored, luxurious foyer. Inside, the air was cool and crisp, with a faint scent of polished wood and pricey cologne. Every detail exuded wealth and distinction, from the exquisite furniture to the enormous chandelier suspended from the ceiling. Freya walked to the front desk, her heels clicking lightly on the floor.

"Yes, good afternoon," she said, her voice coming out weaker than she intended as she approached the receptionist. "I'm here to see Mr. Kingsman."

The receptionist, a woman with perfectly styled hair and a sharp, tailored suit, had a cold, appraising gaze. Her face was unreadable, but the slight curvature of her lip indicated disapproval.

"Name?" the receptionist inquired in a clipped, indifferent voice, as if speaking to someone far beneath her.

Her chest tightened, but she tried to keep her voice calm as she answered, "Freya Blackwood."

The receptionist's manicured fingers shuffled through a stack of papers, her eyes scanning the list until she paused. A single eyebrow arched in mild surprise as she found Freya's name. Distaste laced her voice when she spoke again, as though Freya's presence was an inconvenience.

"Elevator on the left," she said curtly, handing over a sleek black ID card with the words "Special Guest" embossed in gold lettering.

Freya took the card with a hurried, whispered, "Thank you," and quickly walked toward the elevators, her heart thudding in her chest. She could feel the receptionist's eyes lingering on her back, and the weight of that judgment made her steps feel heavier.

As she neared the elevators, a uniformed guard stood there. He gave a short bow, acknowledging her, and stepped forward to open the elevator doors for her. The guard pressed a button for the top floor, and Freya could see herself twitching a little, her nervous expression reflected back at her from the smooth, mirrored walls.

Freya took a deep breath as the elevator began to rise and the quiet hum of the machinery filled the room. She glanced down at the Special Guest ID in her hand, her fingers brushing over the raised letters. Alphonse Kingsman's world was different, she realized. Here, status meant everything, and she was about to step into his domain.

As the elevator climbed higher, her stomach tightened with anticipation, each passing second bringing her closer to him, to whatever awaited her in that office perched at the top of the magnificent tower.

The top level offered a stunning outlook. When Freya emerged from the elevator, she was astounded by the room's magnificence. The polished wood floors and the warm, inviting lighting created a cozy, businesslike atmosphere throughout the space. It felt like it was from the bustling city below.

Ahead of her, a woman who sat at a small desk looked up and smiled—a stark contrast to the cold reception she had received downstairs. This woman was older, her smile kind and welcoming.

She got up and said kindly, "You must be Miss Blackwood. I am Lydia Stall, the assistant of Mr. Kingsman. Mr. Kingsman is anticipating your arrival." She pointed to two stately wooden doors, their dark oak glittering in the dim light.

Freya nodded her thanks, her heart beating faster with each step she took toward the doors. As the woman opened them and closed them behind her, Freya stepped into Alphonse Kingsman's office.

The room did not disappoint.

It was a reflection of the man himself—beautiful, elegant, and meticulously organized. The city skyline was breathtakingly visible from a wall of broad, floor-to-ceiling windows that faced a spacious couch with a sleek coffee table. Beside the couch, near the windows, was a big desk. The wall behind it was lined with books, folders, and other resources, all of which were precisely placed to show the man's strength.

And there, sitting at the desk, was Alphonse Kingsman— the reason for her nervousness. His suit jacket was draped over the back of his chair, and he was seated in his button-up shirt, the sleeves rolled up to his elbows. He looked effortlessly powerful, gracefully shifting between papers that lay on his sleek, state-of-the-art laptop.

He didn't bother looking up when she entered the room. Instead, he continued working, his voice cutting through the silence with an air of authority. "You can sit."

Freya was startled for a moment, her heart racing as she blushed slightly. His commanding presence always had a way of unsettling her. She nodded quickly and moved to the couch, dropping her bag to the floor, careful not to let her bulky, old laptop make too much noise.

As she settled into her seat, Alphonse stood up from his desk and walked toward her with a stack of documents in his hand. Each of his movements was deliberate and controlled, and it was impossible to shake the memory of their last encounter in the conference room—the way he'd made her feel and the unspoken tension that lingered.

She scolded herself for feeling nervous, for letting his presence get to her. *Why am I like this?* Could it be that deep down, she was expecting something from him? Could it be that she was anticipating something beyond mere professionalism? She hated to admit it, but after what had happened in the conference room, she wasn't sure where their relationship stood. Was Alphonse capable of keeping things strictly professional?

"Here are the files I want you to revise first," he said coolly, handing her the stack of documents. His tone was as detached as ever, yet there was something in the way he held her gaze for just a moment longer than necessary.

Freya nodded, taking the folder from him and placing it on her lap. Trying to maintain a steady tone, she replied, "I'll make sure to go over them thoroughly."

As her other hand reached into her purse for her laptop, it felt even more outdated in the sleek, modern environment of his office. The screen flickered to life with a faint hum as she set it on the coffee table. Alphonse's eyes flickered to her laptop for a moment, a faint trace of confusion crossing his otherwise unreadable expression. He didn't say anything, but Freya could feel his curiosity as he glanced at the old device. Before she could make any comment, he turned back to his desk, shifting his attention back to his work.

Freya frowned slightly, her mind still puzzling over the situation. Usually, when she worked with high-profile clients like this, they'd send representatives or employees to handle paperwork.

She half-expected Alphonse to pass her off to a company employee, to whom he was supposed to delegate mundane tasks, but was not receiving the expected support from someone lower in the hierarchy. But instead, here he was, personally handing her the documents. She couldn't shake the feeling that something was off.

Unable to control her curiosity, she found herself asking, "Why are you reviewing these yourself?"

Alphonse halted, turned to her, and fixed his piercing blue gaze on her. The tension between them increased for a moment, his intense gaze making her heart race.

"I don't trust others with this," he said simply, his voice cold but firm.

Freya tilted her head. Don't trust others? The words echoed in her mind, and as she stared back at him, she realized something far deeper might be at play. Was this an excuse to keep her close, or was there something else going on behind the scenes? Could he be investigating his own company from within?

The thought hit her like a shockwave, and she gasped softly. Could Alphonse be experiencing trust issues with his own company? The idea appeared nearly unfeasible, yet Kingsman Enterprises was a vast empire, brimming with the kind of power and secrets that would captivate anyone. If there was something happening beneath the surface, something internal, it would explain why he wanted to keep certain matters under his direct control.

Alphonse's voice broke the atmosphere in the room before she could delve any deeper into her thoughts. "You're the best in the company, in my opinion."

Incredulous at the unexpected compliment, Freya blinked. It might have sounded like flattery coming from anyone else, but it meant something to Alphonse. There was no room for exaggeration or politeness with him. He said only what he meant.

"I..." she stammered, trying to process everything. "Thank you, sir."

Alphonse's gaze lingered on her for a moment longer, his expression unreadable, before he turned back to his desk. Freya watched him, thoughts and questions racing through her head.

It was obvious that she was now in the center of whatever was going on at Kingsman Enterprises.

She couldn't help but wonder how deep these thoughts went as she returned her focus to the folder in front of her.

CHAPTER ELEVEN

Freya was so engrossed in the documents in front of her that she didn't notice how much time had passed. The sun had settled, leaving the sky bathed in deep hues of blue, and night had fallen over the city. The office was now bathed in the soft glow of the city lights shining through the massive windows. It wasn't until the faint smell of cigarette smoke filled the air that she looked up, her thoughts suddenly broken by the scent.

Alphonse was standing in front of the window, the city skyline framing his silhouette. He was smoking a cigarette slowly while holding it to his lips with one hand casually tucked into his pocket. His subtle, easygoing posture emphasized his broad shoulders, strong jawline, and command of the room without a word. Freya's gaze lingered on him for an extended period, her thoughts drifting before she could control herself.

He was undeniably handsome. Perfect, even. He was flawless in every aspect that mattered. "Like what you see?"

His voice, low and edged with amusement, snapped her out of her trance. Freya's cheeks began to burn as her face flushed instantly. She fumbled with her laptop and shut it quickly. She was mortified to discover that someone had noticed her staring.

"I should go; it's late," she muttered as she clumsily gathered her belongings. Trying not to show it, she stuffed her laptop and papers into her bag with clumsy hands. She became even more agitated when she sensed that he was observing her with a hint of amusement.

A gentle hand stopped her as she was about to leave, slinging her bag over her shoulder. She froze at the warmth of his touch on her arm. She could feel the heat radiating from his body because he was now standing directly next to her. His presence was overwhelming, and she felt her knees weaken as he gazed at her intensely.

"Take them off."

Freya blinked, her breath hitching. Her mind scrambled to catch up. "W-what?" she stammered, unsure if she had heard him correctly. Excuse me?

But Alphonse didn't wait for a response. Alphonse extended his hand, smoothly sliding it over her thigh, causing Freya's breath to become trapped in her throat. She should have moved, should have protested, but she was frozen, cursed by the way her body responded to his touch. His fingers slid under her skirt, deliberate and confident, grazing over the curve of her ass as he tugged at the hem of her underwear.

With a single tug, he pulled her panties down between her legs in a single fluid motion, leaving her completely exposed. Her thoughts raced. How on earth does he manage to do that so easily? She bit her lip in thought, finding it difficult to comprehend what had happened.

A smirk played at the corner of his lips. He knew exactly what he was doing, and worse, he knew the effect he had on her. She could feel the heat rise to her face, and worse, the growing wetness between her legs. Her body was betraying her, and he could see it—she knew he could.

Freya averted her gaze, trying to hide her embarrassment, but there was no hiding what had just happened. Her underwear, now wet with her arousal, was pooled at her feet, a silent testament to how easily her body had surrendered to him.

"César is waiting for you downstairs to take you home," Alphonse said coolly, as though the circumstance was nothing out of the ordinary. His voice was calm and authoritative. "You may go."

Freya forced herself to look at him, trying to gather whatever dignity she had left. Despite the tightness in her throat, she mustered the courage to look him in the eye for a brief moment. She let out a sharp sigh, turned away, stepped out of her now-discarded underwear, and picked up her bag.

She walked towards the door, her thoughts scattered and her heart pounding. But just before she stepped out, she caught a glimpse of him out of the corner of her eye. Alphonse bent down, casually picking up her discarded underwear with a satisfied grin on his face.

"Fucking perv," she thought, biting her lip as she left the office, the door clicking shut behind her.

***

The remainder of the week went smoothly, which was a pleasant diversion from the conflict that had characterized her earlier encounters with Alphonse. By immersing herself in the copious amounts of documentation that Kingsman had supplied, Freya was able to maintain a professional demeanor. She put forth a lot of effort in her work, while Natasha and Elihaj, assigned to other tasks, kept the rest of the team focused on their clients. After all, Kingsman had been clear—he wanted as few people involved as possible.

Now, Freya found herself back in Alphonse's office, doing her best to maintain her composure as the day stretched on. She glanced at her watch. It was already 4 p.m., and she realized she hadn't seen Alphonse take a single break for food. How does he function without eating? She wondered, feeling her hunger gnawing at her.

Needing a moment away from the mounting tension, Freya excused herself to the bathroom. About 25 minutes later, she returned, relieved to find Lydia from earlier standing by the door, clutching two takeout bags.

"Miss Blackwood, they left these items for you," she said, smiling courteously.

Freya said, "Thank you" and took the bags from her, setting them on the coffee table. As soon as she put her laptop down, the room filled with the aroma of freshly prepared, delectable meals. Freya's stomach growled softly, grateful for the ordered meal.

Alphonse, who had been completely engrossed in his work, looked up from his desk with a faintly wary expression. His sharp eyes softened slightly as the smell of the food reached him, and Freya couldn't help but notice how his nose twitched at the scent.

"I haven't seen you eat anything all day, and I figured you might need to eat," she said, trying to keep her tone light as she pulled the takeout containers from the bags. She opened one of the foam containers and gestured toward him. "I've got enough for us both."

Alphonse's face flashed with a hint of amusement as he raised an eyebrow. With a faint grin tugging at the corner of his lips, he questioned, "You call this dinner?"

Freya's irritation flared at his contemptuous tone. "Call it whatever you want," she said, her voice firm, though she softened it with a smile. "I'm just being modest, Alphonse."

As soon as the name slipped out, casual and unguarded, Freya tensed. She could feel his gaze sharpen, and for a moment, the air between them shifted. Her heart pounded at the intensity with which his blue eyes examined her. Alphonse got up, rolled up his sleeves, and walked across the room toward her without saying anything. He took a seat beside her on the couch, his movements purposeful but his face unreadable.

Now that he was sitting next to her, the room seemed more intimate and smaller, and the tension that had been there was still present. Freya gave him one of the containers, and they were silent for a while. With the exception of the occasional shuffle as they rearranged their plates and the gentle sounds of forks scraping against plastic, they started eating in silence.

As they ate, Freya couldn't help but glance at him. The moment felt strangely domestic, as though their typical dynamic had lifted. The strong CEO who ruled the room with cold authority was no longer there; instead, he appeared more genuine and human.

However, Freya was unable to overcome the underlying tension in spite of the calm. Ever-present in the back of her mind was the memory of their previous encounters—the conference room, his silent orders, the way he made her feel.

After they had eaten, Alphonse leaned back a little and looked out the window, taking in the view of the city below.

"Thank you," he said softly, without the usual abrasiveness in his voice.

Startled by how straightforward his appreciation was, Freya blinked. For a second, she wasn't sure how to react because she hadn't anticipated it.

At last, she said softly, "You're welcome," and started packing up the empty containers.

They were silent for a long time, but it wasn't awkward. Rather, it was full of an implicit understanding—the kind of moment in which words were not required.

And that was fine with Freya for once.

***

Lydia, Alphonse's assistant, gave Freya a small, anxious smile when she arrived at Kingsman Enterprises and then opened the door to his office. She told her that Mr. Kingsman was running a bit behind schedule. "You can wait inside. He will arrive soon."

With a nod of gratitude, Freya entered the office, her shoulders hurting from carrying her laptop and the folders she had been carrying all day. Finally able to unwind, she sighed with relief as she sank into the couch. She was thankful that the meetings had been professional throughout the week. Even so, there was an unmistakable tension in her body, an almost restless energy that had nothing to do with her job.

Really, it was ironic. Freya had never considered herself sexually inclined. She actually believed that part of her apathy had pushed Lucas to look for fulfillment with someone else. But here she was, yearning to relive those intense, unnerving moments, longing for the memory of her encounter with Alphonse. With a deep sigh, she leaned back on the couch and gave herself permission to indulge in her thoughts for a moment.

Peace was short-lived.

The door slammed open with a loud thud, almost causing Freya to jump out of her body. Alphonse barged in, his normally cool and collected expression turned to one of terror as his face twisted in rage. With a loud bang that reverberated throughout the room, the door slammed behind him. He was unlike anything Freya had ever seen. Normally calm and collected, his presence now exuded a strength that thickened the tension in the air.

He strode over to the table by the windows where he kept his liquor in reserve and silently poured himself a drink. As if the anger were physically weighing him down, his broad shoulders were tense, and every movement was sharp. Freya's heart was pounding as she watched, not knowing what to do. Is she supposed to excuse herself and go? Before she could make a decision, his voice broke the silence.

He asked in a low, clipped voice, with his back to her, "How are we doing with the information?" He drained his drink quickly and then poured another for himself.

Freya swallowed and tried not to sound intimidated as she answered, trying to steady her voice. "For the higher-ups you mentioned, I have been examining the financial flow, expense, and stock trend data. The reported numbers appear to be inconsistent, especially when it comes to the distribution of bonuses among specific executives and the acquisition of opulent assets. The expenses don't match the income flows… It's almost like some are manipulating their stock options to create loopholes for personal gain."

She watched him as she continued, trying to gauge his reaction. He didn't turn around, but she could see his knuckles whitening as he gripped the glass tighter.

"It's subtle, but the discrepancies are noticeable when you compare the timing of stock dips and the expenses these executives are reporting. It's possible they're hiding their movements through third-party accounts," she added, trying to keep her explanation clear.

For the next fifteen minutes, Freya answered his questions, doing her best to stay focused while he poured drink after drink. The undercurrent of anger persisted, but by the time he finished his fifth glass, his shoulders appeared to have relaxed. He finally turned, walking back to his desk and sitting down, the tension easing just a little.

As she wrapped up her discussion, Freya began typing something on her laptop, her fingers working over the old keyboard, when Alphonse's voice cut through the silence again.

"Come over here."

The words were straightforward but unambiguous. A little taken aback by the abrupt order, Freya looked up, but she had no intention of disobeying him. Uncertain of what he wanted, she got up from the couch and approached him, her heart racing.

Alphonse pushed his chair away from his desk as she walked up, then quickly pulled her onto his lap. Startled by the sudden intimacy of the gesture, Freya gasped, her body going rigid for a moment before she slumped back against his chest. His powerful arms encircled her waist, his grip firm but not tight. As though her presence was calming him, he leaned in close and exhaled deeply, his breath warm against her neck.

"The bastards think they can skim off the top. They'll learn," he muttered, his lips dangerously close to her ear. His tone was low. A mix of rage and something more sinister that made her skin crawl. "I'll hold them accountable."

Freya's heart raced as his hand slid over her thigh, his fingers tracing patterns over the fabric of her skirt. She inhaled sharply, feeling the heat of his touch as it settled at the top of her thigh.

There was a pause, and then a low chuckle escaped his lips. "No underwear?"

Freya flushed, her face turning a deep shade of red. She cursed herself for not thinking to wear something beneath her skirt after their previous encounters. Trying to maintain some dignity, she shot him an exasperated look. *"You're costing me a fortune in lingerie,"* she protested, sounding offended and embarrassed at the same time.

The office was filled with the rich, real sound of Alphonse's laughter. Freya caught a glimpse of the man behind the cold exterior, and for the first time she saw something lighter in him. His laugh was deep and unguarded, and the tension between them temporarily vanished.

Freya thought it was the most exquisite laugh she had ever heard him make.

She couldn't resist grinning as she felt the situation become almost unreal: she was sitting on the lap of the most incredibly strong man she had ever encountered, yet he appeared human in this moment. Fun, even.

"Tsk, tsk," he murmured, his voice low and dangerous as his hand pressed firmly against her trembling thighs. "I might have to punish you."

His fingers found her clit; her skirt bunched up around her hips. The sudden pressure made her gasp, a moan escaping before she could bite it back. Hastily, she caught herself, teeth sinking into her bottom lip, trying to regain control.

"Did you miss me, kitty?" She was trying desperately to hold back the moans bubbling up in her throat. "Ah ah," Alphonse teased, his voice laced with amusement. "No holding back. I want to hear you."

One hand worked between her legs, rubbing her slick folds with maddening precision, while the other slipped beneath her bra, teasing her sensitive nipples. She could feel the wetness soaking through his pants, her body pressed back against his hard chest. His erection pressed insistently against her, the sensation heightening her desperation.

Her body trembled, yet she clung to what little pride remained, biting her lip in a futile attempt to keep quiet. However, Alphonse persisted, cruelly torturing her with his fingers, evoking her pleasure with each playful flick. Her body has become a traitorous thing. She was determined not to break and give him the satisfaction he craved.

Then, without warning, he pushed three fingers inside her, curling them and twisting against her walls, and a loud, desperate moan escaped her lips before she could stop it. "That's it, Little Kitty. Moan for me."

For what felt like a blissful eternity, Alphonse kept up the assault as she teetered on the edge, her moans spilling freely now.

"You want me?" His lips nipped her earlobe as he growled into her ear.

Without warning, he grabbed her, flipping her over his desk with a swift motion, pinning her flat on her stomach. In one fluid, brutal thrust, he was inside her. Freya cried out, her fingers grasping the edges of the table as her body clenched around him. Alphonse groaned, low and deep, his hips pressing hard into her as he filled her completely.

It became a rhythm—a dance of thrusts and moans. Freya's body tightened around Alphonse with an orgasm that crashed over her; every time she felt him respond in kind, his groans turned guttural as he quickened his pace, clearly reveling in every second. Her body completely surrendered to his as their movements synchronized in an unspoken, frenzied pleasure.

Alphonse smirked with satisfaction as he sat back in his chair after she had finally caught her breath, her pulse still pounding. In a low, languid voice, he muttered, "That was... relaxing."

Freya was about to stand, her legs trembling, but before she could move, his hand pressed down on her back, keeping her in place. "Stay."

Her breath hitched as she glanced over her shoulder, watching as Alphonse calmly opened one of his drawers and pulled out a packet of wipes. Without a word, he wiped her clean—his hands gentle, reverent even. The same hands that had just pinned her now treated her like porcelain. She had braced for cruelty but found care instead—the contradiction making her stomach flip. When he was done, he stood, pulling her up with him, smoothing her skirt back into its proper place, restoring her appearance like nothing had happened.

"Freshen up," he said, nodding toward the door concealed behind the wall of books. His tone was matter-of-fact, but there was a glint of amusement in his eyes as he opened another drawer and pulled out a fresh pair of pants.

Freya blinked, still piecing together what was happening. "Why?" she asked, a touch of disbelief in her voice.

Alphonse let his pants drop to the floor, his bare, muscular frame once again stealing her focus as he caught her staring. A smug smile curled at the edge of his lips as he stepped into the new pants, pulling them on casually.

"We're going to a real dinner," he said, buttoning his pants with a smirk, leaving her speechless.

CHAPTER TWELVE

Freya sat in the backseat of the sleek, black car, staring out the window as the city lights blurred by. She had genuinely attempted to refuse, and she had indeed done so. But the moment Alphonse had fixed her with that cold, piercing stare—the one that left no room for argument—she knew she had lost. She had sighed in resignation and agreed to the dinner, though a part of her still felt unsure.

The car parked in front of a fancy restaurant with finely detailed interiors that radiated luxury. The exterior was illuminated by soft, golden lights that emphasized the intricate architecture. Freya had never visited this location before. She suddenly felt underdressed, even though she had assumed that her sleek black pencil skirt and gray blouse were appropriate for a business meeting.

Even as he stepped out of a car, Alphonse's presence was commanding, and he was the first to depart. He was dressed in his favorite dark suit, the form-fitting fabric of which complemented his toned figure perfectly. In contrast to his cool confidence, Freya felt a twinge of nervousness as she followed him out of the car.

Alphonse held out a hand to Freya as a valet met them and took the car. After a moment of hesitation, she took it. The warmth of Alphonse's hand enveloped hers as they entered the eatery. The ambiance inside was magnificent, with dim lighting, mellow background music, and the distinct sound of hushed conversations among the affluent guests seated at the tastefully decorated tables.

"Order whatever you'd like," Alphonse said, his voice low and smooth, the kind that seemed to make everything sound like a command. "I'm sure everything here will meet your standards."

Freya raised an eyebrow, almost startled by his words. "Standards?" she echoed, her lips curling slightly. *The soup alone costs more than my monthly bill!*

The waiter approached, and Freya scanned the menu quickly. The steak alone costs as much as her mortgage payment. She would rather not seem rattled, especially not in front of Alphonse, who seemed entirely at ease. The waiter hovered expectantly, and Freya could feel Alphonse's gaze burning into her. She fidgeted slightly, her fingers gripping the edges of the menu.

At last, her voice was hardly audible above a whisper, "Please, the steak." She glanced up at Alphonse, hoping he wouldn't catch her discomfort.

Alphonse, still smirking, gave his order with his usual confidence before handing his menu to the waiter. As soon as the waiter left, Freya shifted in her seat, feeling the weight of the moment settle over her like a thick fog.

"You don't have to be so troubled," Alphonse said smoothly, his tone carrying that same mixture of amusement and command. "You've earned your invitation, so I'm inviting you here."

Exhaling, Freya tried to calm herself. "It's not every day that I'm invited to a place where a soup costs more than my monthly bills. It is overwhelming."

Alphonse's face softened, but his intense stare remained unwavering. "You'll adjust to it." He spoke quietly but confidently, as though it were a given. Leaning back in his chair, he observed her intently. "You've been performing well."

Freya shrugged, trying to deflect her unease with a small smile. "I'm just doing my job."

He narrowed his eyes, clearly amused by her modesty. "And yet you do it better than most."

Freya raised an eyebrow, her fingers wrapping around the glass of water in front of her. "Double meaning?" she muttered.

Alphonse chuckled softly, the sound low and rich as he took a sip of his whiskey. His voice was smooth and full of unspoken intent as he answered, "Definitely."

Freya's heart began to beat a little quicker as her hand tightened around her glass. Uncertain whether to be intrigued or irritated, tension simmered beneath the surface. Perhaps both.

"Is everything a game to you?" she asked, her tone lighter than the intensity she felt.

Alphonse set his glass down gently, leaning forward just enough to close the space between them. "Not everything," he said, his voice quiet yet powerful. "Just the things that I am certain I can win."

Freya felt the challenge in his eyes, a deliberate provocation that quickened her heartbeat. She was aware that everything about Alphonse contained secrets she wasn't quite ready to know, even though she couldn't help but feel excited to be in his company.

She inhaled, leaned back a little, and forced a smile. "I suppose you enjoy the challenge then," she said, trying to keep her tone casual.

His smile was slow, almost predatory. "I enjoy winning," he corrected, the words laced with certainty.

"Well, I'm interested to see the day you don't win, Mr. Kingsman," Freya said with a teasing smile as she brought her glass of water to her lips.

Before she could take a sip, Alphonse's hand shot out, stopping her glass mid-air. He took the glass from her and carefully put it back on the table, maintaining his piercing gaze. The waiter then approached and placed a green cocktail in front of him. Freya's eyes widened slightly as Alphonse smiled and slid the drink into her hand.

As soon as she smelled the aroma of sweet, fresh melon, she knew it was her favorite—her favorite cocktail

"I always make it a point to learn more."

Freya's heartbeat quickened, and for the first time that evening, she realized just how intricately he was playing this game. And just how deeply she had stepped into it.

***

The tension from the dinner lingered between them as they made their way back to Freya's house in silence. She sat with her heavy laptop and meeting documents in her bag, which was at her feet. She fixed her gaze on the window, observing the flickering city lights in the shadows.

Then, however, she sensed Alphonse's hand on her thigh. It felt as natural as it could be, firm and confident. She looked at him, and her breath caught a little. He seemed at ease, absorbed in his phone, the dim glow of the screen highlighting his keen features. Her heart raced at the contrast between his cool manner and the weight of his hand on her leg.

She didn't move. A part of her wasn't even sure if she wanted to.

When the car finally came to a stop in front of her house, Freya moved to exit, her hand reaching for the door handle. However, a powerful hand stopped her before she could open it, firmly and unquestionably gripping her arm. With such hunger, Alphonse leaned in and pressed his lips to hers, disarming her before she could react.

She was left speechless by the intensity of the kiss, which was strong and unfiltered. With a sense of possession that reverberated throughout her body, his hand moved from her arm to her waist, drawing her in closer as he intensified the kiss. Freya's mind went blank, all thoughts of resistance melting away as her body responded to him, her pulse pounding in her ears.

There was nothing gentle about it. The kiss was a surge of energy, as if Alphonse had been holding back until now, and now that the floodgates were open, there was no stopping it. Freya's body leaned into him as her mind tried to keep up with the intensity of the moment, her hands automatically gripping his suit.

Freya stared at him, utterly shaken, her heart pounding as he finally withdrew, leaving her gasping for air. His gaze was dark, his expression unreadable, but there was a hint of satisfaction in the way his lips curved into a smirk. He didn't say a word, just watched her with those piercing blue eyes, as though daring her to make sense of what had just happened.

Before she could gather her thoughts, Alphonse's hand slipped from her waist, his touch lingering for just a second longer than necessary before he leaned back in his seat.

He said, "Goodnight, Miss Blackwood," in a quiet, low voice, as if nothing out of the ordinary had just happened.

With her heart still racing, Freya swallowed forcefully and reached for the door handle. Her mind spinning from the sheer intensity of what had just happened, she got out of the car and walked up to her house, her legs feeling unsteady.

Freya stood motionless on the sidewalk, watching the car drive away as the taillights faded into the distance. Her lips were still burning, and the cool night air did little to put out the fire in her chest. She pressed her fingers lightly to her mouth, as if confirming it had actually happened.

Confusion, desire, and an inexplicable sense of entrapment whirled through her mind. She did not know how to read it, what it meant for her career and personal life, or how she had allowed herself to reach this point in the first place. But there was no doubt that she had gone too far, or rather that he had pulled her over it, and there was no simple way to turn back.

Freya closed her eyes for a moment, feeling the weight of it all settle over her. The dynamic between them was dangerous and complicated, and every time she thought she had control, Alphonse found a way to pull her deeper into his orbit.

And now, standing alone in the stillness of the night, she understood one thing with startling clarity: whatever this situation was, she was in it now. And there was no way out.

***

The house was still when Freya entered, the door shutting softly behind her. She exhaled, kicking off her heels, already halfway toward her room when—

"Who was that?"

The voice halted her movement.

She turned to find Lucas, half-hidden in the hallway shadows, arms crossed, brow furrowed. The glow from the kitchen caught just enough of his face to show the tension building behind his eyes.

Oh, we're doing this? Now?

"A client," she said coolly. "He offered to drop me off after dinner."

"At eleven p.m.?" he stepped forward. "You never stay out this late for meetings."

Freya let out a worn sigh, moving past him toward the living room. "We had drinks after. That's all."

"Drinks," Lucas echoed, his tone tightening. "So you're just... out with other men now? Is that what we're doing?"

Her jaw clenched.

Says the man who's been cheating behind my back
for God knows how long.

But she didn't say it. She wouldn't give him that power. Not tonight.

"It was work," she snapped. "I'm not doing this with you right now."

She started walking toward the couch, rummaging for her laptop, ready to escape this conversation in the only way she could—burying herself in work.

But Lucas reached out, grabbing her arm to stop her.

"Freya, stop."

His grip wasn't painful, but it was firm. Too firm. Her arm jerked in his grasp as she tried to shake him off.

"Let go of me," she said, voice low, warning sharp.

"You're just going to walk away? You don't even talk to me anymore—"

"Maybe because there's nothing left to say!"

She twisted to pull away again, her frustration rising like a fever. Lucas's eyes searched hers wildly—his anger tangled with desperation.

And then—he kissed her.

Freya froze for a heartbeat—shocked, disgusted, stunned.

What the hell—

She shoved at his chest with both hands, recoiling from the heat of his mouth.

"Don't you dare—!"

As she pushed, the strap of her bag slipped from her shoulder. Her heavy laptop rolled out of it. She stepped back instinctively—right onto a loose rug. Her heel twisted. The ground vanished.

And then—

CRACK.

Her ribs slammed into the sharp corner of the coffee table. The impact stole her breath. She collapsed hard onto the floor, the laptop clattering beside her, the screen shattered.

"Freya!" Lucas dropped down beside her, wide-eyed, panic crashing into his features. But she recoiled violently, curling away from his hands.

"Don't touch me!" She gasped, arms wrapped tight around her side, every breath a stab of fire.

"It's late; I was worried," he stammered.

"Stop talking." Her voice shook, but her eyes were like ice. Lucas froze, his hand suspended uselessly in the air.

"Freya, I swear, I didn't mean to hurt you—"

"But you did." Her voice cracked with anger. "You always do."

She sat up slowly, bracing herself against the couch, wincing as pain flared along her ribs. Her jaw clenched tight as she blinked back the spinning sensation.

Lucas knelt there, helpless, guilt plastered across his face.

"Let me help you—"

"No."

She stood shaky and breathless and took a single step away from him.

"I don't want your help. I don't want your apologies. I want space."

He didn't move. He made no attempt to stop her this time.

Freya looked down at the shattered laptop, the scattered pages on the floor, and the cracked edges of a relationship long past saving. She didn't even glance at him again.

She turned and walked down the hallway, each breath laced with pain, each step a choice not to collapse.

Stopping now would prevent her from leaving.

CHAPTER THIRTEEN

Moonlight gilded the estate, firelight licking across books and an untouched bourbon at the desk—yet none of it reached Alphonse.

She was stunning, undeniably so. The woman stood near the doorway, her figure illuminated by the soft light. Her dress clung to her curves, chosen to entice, and her sultry smile suggested confidence in her ability to captivate. As she stepped further into the room, her heels made barely a sound on the polished wood floor.

"You seem… distracted," she said, her voice smooth, her gaze fixed on him. She approached slowly, her hand brushing over the back of the leather chair. "Something on your mind?"

Alphonse barely looked up, his dark eyes focused on the fire. "Work," he replied curtly, though his thoughts were far from the deals and numbers that usually consumed him.

She smiled, undeterred. "Let me help you forget," she purred, stepping closer. She placed a hand on his shoulder, her nails lightly tracing the line of his collarbone. "You don't have to act like Alphonse Kingsman tonight."

He didn't pull away, but his lack of response was telling. His mind was already elsewhere, consumed by thoughts of Freya—her quiet determination, her defiant independence, and the way her presence seemed to disrupt his carefully ordered world.

The paid companion took his silence as encouragement and leaned in, her lips brushing against his jawline. "You don't need to think," she whispered, her fingers sliding down the front of his shirt. "Just let me—"

"Stop," Alphonse said, his voice low but commanding. He reached up, catching her wrists gently but firmly. His gaze finally lifted to meet hers, steady and unyielding. "That's enough."

Her brows furrowed, confusion flashing across her face. "Did I do something wrong?"

He shook his head, standing and guiding her back a step. "No," he said, his tone quiet but distant. "You're perfect. But your response isn't what I need."

The woman blinked, her professional demeanor slipping for a moment. "Mr. Kingsman, I can—"

"No," he interrupted firmly. He pulled open a drawer and retrieved a sleek leather wallet. Removing an amount of cash more than sufficient, he handed it to her. "Take the night off. Thank Veronica for her choices."

She hesitated, then forced a polite smile. "If you change your mind—"

He shook his head, already turning to open the double doors of the study. The estate's vast hallway stretched out before them, dimly lit by antique sconces. "I won't. Have a good night."

The woman stepped through the door, her heels clicking softly against the tiled floor as she disappeared into the shadows. Alphonse closed the doors behind her, the latch clicking into place, and leaned against the cool wood for a moment, exhaling slowly.

The house felt oppressively quiet, despite its grandeur. Alphonse strode back to the desk, but the bourbon no longer tempted him. His thoughts remained stubbornly locked on Freya—the way she met his gaze without flinching, the fire in her voice when she stood her ground, and the way she occupied his mind without trying.

Sinking into the leather chair, Alphonse stared into the fire. For the first time in years, the distraction of company and indulgence wasn't enough. Freya had upended something in him, something he couldn't ignore, and it left him feeling both uneasy and exhilarated.

He loosened his tie, staring into the flames as they danced, casting fleeting shadows. Alphonse Kingsman, the man in charge of everything, was left wondering if he was prepared to lose this game, as Freya had already infiltrated his life in unique ways.

***

Freya sat stiffly on the edge of the couch, her posture tense, one arm subtly bracing her side. Each breath sent a dull pulse of pain through her ribs, but she forced herself to stay composed. She pulled a folder from her bag, teeth clenched as she tried not to wince with every movement.

Across the room, Alphonse stood near the floor-to-ceiling window, outlined by the last light of day. A glass of whiskey sat in his hand, his gaze fixed on the skyline.

Then he turned. His sharp blue eyes landed on her—focused, observant. He noticed the missing laptop immediately.

"Where's your laptop?" he asked, calm but unmistakably precise.

Freya swallowed hard, shifting uncomfortably. "I had an accident with it," she said softly, trying to keep her voice steady and neutral.

Alphonse quickly placed his drink on the table and took out his phone. His expression didn't change as he pulled out his phone, dialed quickly, and spoke into the receiver

"César," he said smoothly, "bring a new laptop. She'll need it by morning."

Freya blinked. "No, wait—Alphonse, you don't have to—"

She stood too quickly. Pain ripped through her side like lightning. Her balance faltered; her vision swam.

But before gravity could win, Alphonse caught her.

He was across the room in seconds, hands strong and steady, gripping her waist with startling care. He guided her back to the couch with an almost possessive protectiveness.

"I'm fine," Freya whispered, but her voice betrayed her.

Alphonse did not accept her words without question. With a swift, decisive motion, he crouched down in front of her, his eyes narrowing as he gently lifted the hem of her shirt.

He saw them. The bruises on her side were already turning dark, a harsh reminder of her fall against the coffee table. The swollen marks stood out against her skin, and Freya felt a fresh wave of embarrassment and vulnerability wash over her as Alphonse examined the injury.

His face changed. He was no longer the calm, unbothered executive. Now he was all steel and fury.

"What happened?" he asked, voice low and lethal.

"It's nothing," Freya murmured, attempting to pull her shirt back down, but Alphonse's hand gently but firmly stopped her.

"What. Happened?" His tone sharpened, slicing through her evasion.

She could lie. She could tell him it was nothing. But something in his stare told her he'd know the truth anyway. "Lucas and I argued. He attempted to kiss me, and I pushed him away. I fell."

Alphonse's grip on her shoulder tightened ever so slightly as he processed her words, his eyes narrowing as he drew in a slow breath, but she felt the tremor in his restraint. Alphonse's jaw tightened, and his eyes darkened further. He didn't say anything at first, but the silence was thick with anger, his expression hardening as the meaning of her words sank in.

"He did this to you?" he asked, his voice a growl just beneath the surface.

Freya opened her mouth to say something, to try and downplay the situation, "I mean, it wasn't on purpose."

But he didn't look convinced. He stood slowly, and the silence that followed was heavy.

"I'll handle it," he said finally.

"Alphonse—"

He held up a hand, silencing her. His gaze softened for just a breath, but the fire behind it didn't dim.

He picked up his phone again. "Lydia, call Dr. Hudson. Now."

Freya opened her mouth to protest, but she knew it was useless. Alphonse was not inclined to overlook such situations. She sat back against the couch, still clutching her side, feeling the throbbing pain in her ribs. A few minutes later, Dr. Hudson arrived—salt-and-pepper hair, calm eyes, professional but kind. He examined her carefully, taking in the bruises with clinical efficiency.

"No fractures," he said. "But deep bruising. You'll be sore for a while. Pain meds and rest."

He handed her a prescription, patted her hand gently, and then gave a respectful nod to Alphonse. "Take care of her, Mr. Kingsman."

Alphonse nodded quietly.

When the doctor left, Freya finally broke the silence. "You didn't have to do all this."

"I did," he said simply.

She exhaled. "You don't have to fix everything."

Alphonse walked to the bar, poured another two fingers of whiskey, and leaned back on the edge of his desk. He watched her for a long, unreadable moment.

"I'll have César drive you home," he added. "Rest the weekend. I'll see you Monday."

She nodded, but her chest was tight—not just from bruises, but from the weight of everything she couldn't say. She stood slowly, gathering herself, and walked to the door.

She felt his eyes on her the whole way. The moment the door clicked shut behind her, Alphonse set his glass down with a quiet finality.

His jaw clenched. Lucas had stepped over a boundary. This is a line he couldn't walk back from. In his world, safety meant control. Freya's well-being had been disrupted, and it was clear he wasn't willing to let that go unpunished. The matter wouldn't go unaddressed, and Lucas would know that hurting Freya came with consequences—consequences Alphonse would personally ensure.

Alphonse reached into his inner coat pocket and pulled out his phone.

"Yes, Boss?" A voice answered—rough, thick with a New York accent.

Alphonse's voice was low and cold. "Find Lucas Grant. Don't touch him yet. I want to decide how this ends."

CHAPTER FOURTEEN

Sitting in the hotel lobby, Lucas nervously tapped his foot on the marble floor. The location was upscale—too upscale for his taste—but he hadn't questioned it when Angelica had called to ask to meet here. Their relationship began with a dating app, and they had been acquainted for nearly a year. It wasn't love; it wasn't even emotional. It was purely physical—a convenient escape from the growing tension at home with Freya.

He sighed, frustration gnawing at him. He cared about Freya; he really did, but things between them had become so cold, so distant. The last few months felt hollow and superficial, and the absence of intimacy only worsened it. Freya refused his help, and Lucas knew she was too stubborn to accept anything from him. He'd left a note before he left, using work as an excuse. Angelica was always there to distract him when he needed it.

Angelica is a charming flirt. Brown eyes and honey-blonde waves, and her flawless style strikes a balance between playfulness and sophistication. Upon her arrival, she was swift and concise.

She didn't say hello. Simply walked. Lucas frowned but didn't question it, following her through the restaurant and into the more private, reserved dining areas of the hotel. She guided him through the hall, her steps hurried, until they reached the last room.

Angelica opened the door and gestured for him to enter. The room looked like a corporate conference space, arranged like a private dining area—no doubt the kind of room used for high-profile business dinners. However, what truly surprised

Lucas was the man who stood by the window, his back facing him.

The man wore a dark, well-tailored suit that was spotless and gave off an air of authority. He stood outside facing the in-house garden in a relaxed yet commanding stance. He held a glass of dark liquor in one hand and had a cigarette hanging from the other.

"I apologize for this," Angelica muttered, her voice barely above a whisper. Lucas barely had time to process her words before she slipped out of the room, the door closing softly behind her, leaving him alone with the stranger. A red light blinked above the door—camera disabled.

The man didn't turn immediately. Instead, he spoke in a low, dark tone that shivered through Lucas. "It's impressive how much people are willing to do for money." The man finished his cigarette, placing it calmly in the ashtray on the table behind him. As he turned, Lucas finally got a clear view of his face, and his stomach dropped.

Alphonse Kingsman.

He had seen this man in magazines and heard endless gossip about him at work. Alphonse Kingsman was a name everyone knew—ruthless in business, feared by rivals, and envied by men. You would rather not be in the same room with him, let alone on his bad side.

Lucas's throat became dry. *What the hell is going on?* He opened his mouth to speak, but before he could, Alphonse's voice cut through the silence again.

"Lucas Grant," Alphonse said fluidly, his sharp blue eyes focusing on Lucas as if he were assessing a potential victim.

A chill of uneasiness crept over Lucas. He wasn't prepared for this degree of acquaintance. He started, "Uh, yeah—," but Alphonse went on.

"Born August sixth. Horizon Group, four years. Small title, big mouth."

Lucas swallowed hard, his mind racing. Alphonse wasn't just reciting facts. There was something far more sinister behind this meeting.

"It's been eight months since you've been fucking around with Miss Garner," Alphonse said, his voice now laced with quiet menace.

The words struck Lucas deeply. He froze, his blood running cold. He had tried to keep his encounters with Angelica discreet, careful not to let anyone find out, least of all Freya. But here was Alphonse Kingsman, casually throwing out details like they were written on a file, like he knew everything.

Lucas felt the walls closing in, the room suddenly too small. He needed to play this carefully. This was Alphonse Kingsman, after all. One wrong move, one wrong word, and there would be consequences. He could feel the power radiating off of him, and he wasn't foolish enough to underestimate what Kingsman was capable of.

"I—I don't know what you've heard," Lucas stammered, trying to find his footing, "but—"

Alphonse held up a hand, cutting him off. His eyes darkened as he leaned forward slightly, his expression growing more dangerous by the second. " Mr. Grant. I don't *hear* things. I *know* things."

Lucas's heart pounded in his chest, his mind racing as he tried to figure out how to navigate this situation. He wasn't just dealing with any man—he was dealing with a dangerous man, and he was already at a disadvantage.

"Now," Alphonse continued, his voice chillingly calm, "you and I are going to have a conversation. And by the time we're done, you'll understand exactly what it means to cross paths with me."

Lucas felt his mouth go dry, his hands trembling slightly. He felt a sinking sensation that told him that whatever was going to happen to him would not end well.

His body tensed, as if he were expecting something far worse than what had already been said. Alphonse poured himself another drink with purposeful, almost predatory grace before turning back to face Lucas, who was motionless and unsure how to respond.

"Sit," Alphonse commanded, his hand on the chair beside him. With sweat running down his back, Lucas obeyed.

As Alphonse swirled the amber liquid in his glass, his eyes narrowing slightly as he looked at Lucas with a calculating intensity, the only sound for a moment was the gentle clink of ice. Then Alphonse broke the silence with a slow, deliberate exhale.

He let the ice clink once, like a metronome. "What do you value most in a woman?"

Lucas knew he shouldn't respond to such a seemingly harmless, almost casual question. Beneath the surface, the question feels like a trap. His stomach churned as he tried to understand where the conversation was going.

Alphonse's gaze remained fixed on him, like a predator waiting for its prey to make the wrong move. He was aware that he couldn't afford to respond carelessly.

"I—" Lucas hesitated and had to think. What did Alphonse anticipate as a response? What was he trying to say? He felt the pressure rise as he nervously licked his lips. He spoke slowly, uncertain whether he was expressing what Alphonse wanted to hear, saying, "I value loyalty… trust."

Alphonse's lips curled into a grin, a hint of something sinister appearing on his face as he approached Lucas, his footsteps barely perceptible on the soft carpet. "Loyalty and trust," he said again, quietly, as though he were practicing the words. "Loyalty's a brave word to borrow with your zipper down"

He knew exactly what Alphonse was implying. The accusation about Angelica indicated that Alphonse was toying with him, testing how far he could push him before he broke. He felt as though his every flaw was being scrutinized closely.

"You see," Alphonse continued, his voice a low, dangerous purr, "loyalty and trust are fine values, admirable even. But they only matter if you understand their cost." He leaned in slightly, his cold blue eyes boring into Lucas. "What does loyalty mean to you when you've been betraying the woman you claim to care about? Or is it that you simply value these things only when they suit you?"

Lucas swallowed hard, his face flushing with guilt and anger. Alphonse was aware of the truth, but he still wanted to defend himself and say anything. "I care about Freya," Lucas said quickly, his voice rising in defense. "It's just—things between us have been complicated. I didn't—"

"Stop," Alphonse cut him off, "Don't waste my time with excuses, Mr. Grant."

He stepped closer, towering over him now, his voice low and threatening. "What you value in a woman doesn't matter if you don't understand what it means to respect her." Alphonse's eyes flashed with cold fury. "You say you care for her, but you've proven otherwise."

Lucas clenched his fists at his armrest, feeling trapped. He hadn't expected this confrontation, certainly not from someone like Alphonse Kingsman. He had thought he could handle it, but now, standing before the man who clearly had more control over the situation than him, he now felt small.

"What do you really want from me?" Lucas asked, filled with frustration. "You've made your point."

Alphonse's lips curled into a cold smile, the kind that didn't reach his eyes. "I don't want anything from you, Mr. Grant. You're irrelevant." His words pierced deeply. "What I want is for you to understand the consequences of your actions."

"You have caused harm to Freya," Alphonse added, his tone now menacing. "And I take my contractors' and employees' safety very seriously."

As the realization dawned on Lucas, his blood ran cold and his stomach dropped. Is Alphonse Kingsman Freya's new client?

"Clearly, Mr. Kingsman, there's been a misunderstanding," Lucas stammered, his voice shaking. "It was an accident—"

But before he could finish his sentence, Alphonse moved with terrifying speed. His hand shot out, grabbing Lucas by the back of his head and slamming his face down hard onto the polished surface of the table. The room reverberated with the sickening crack of bone, and Lucas's now-broken nose spat blood.

With his hands flying to his face in an attempt to stop the blood flow, Lucas gasped in agony, the pain blinding him. As he tried to make sense of what had just transpired, his vision swam and his heart raced in sheer terror.

Over him, Alphonse loomed, his icy, unwavering eyes on Lucas like a predator glaring down at its victim. Alphonse calmly spoke, "Don't insult my intelligence, Mr. Grant," as if nothing unusual had just occurred. His tone was cold, and every word pierced the fog of suffering that surrounded Lucas's thoughts.

Panic flooded Lucas's system as his heart raced. Although he could taste the blood in his mouth and feel its sting trickling down his face, the physical pain was far less significant than the fear of Alphonse standing over him. More than just a warning, the gesture was an act of dominance, a reminder that Alphonse had complete control over him.

"I don't care what excuses you make," Alphonse continued, his voice steady, controlled, and terrifyingly calm. "Accident events occur as a result of actions, which are influenced by emotions. Your emotions led you to this point, Mr. Grant."

Lucas, his vision blurred and his body trembling, tried to speak, but all that escaped was a choked gurgle as blood filled his mouth, spilling over his lips. His hands, slick with blood, trembled as he pressed them against his face, his mind struggling to catch up with the brutal reality before him. Every breath was a painful struggle, and fear ran like ice through him.

Alphonse's eyes remained fixed on him, unblinking, as if Lucas's suffering was nothing more than a minor inconvenience. "Freya is a wonderful employee, Mr. Grant," he said, his tone cold and businesslike, as if they were merely discussing work and not the fact that Lucas was bleeding profusely before him. "She's exceptional in her department—dedicated, focused, and valuable."

He paused, his gaze growing more intense. "And I don't want her to be interrupted by people who don't understand the values they claim to hold. People like you betray the loyalty and trust that you expect from others."

Lucas's heart pounded, the pain in his nose and the weight of Alphonse's words crushing him simultaneously. Lucas became more and more aware of his complete helplessness as

Alphonse continued to speak. Not only was Alphonse threatening Lucas, but he was also slowly destroying him.

Alphonse moved closer, his shoes making a gentle clicking sound on the ground as he loomed like a shadow over Lucas. "You'll keep your face out of Freya's life. And you'll keep this off police reports. Consider that mercy."

Lucas attempted to defend himself and seek forgiveness, but his voice once again let him down. His throat constricted, and the overwhelming terror made it impossible to think clearly.

Alphonse leaned slightly closer to Lucas, his icy blue eyes riveting him with a chilling stare. "This could have ended far worse for you."

Lucas's heart pounded in his chest, the words echoing in his mind. He would rather not imagine what that meant in Alphonse's world.

Alphonse straightened up, his expression devoid of emotion, as though the entire violent encounter had already faded from his mind, a minor disturbance in his day. He adjusted his suit with a slow, deliberate motion, his composure unshaken.

"You'll go back to Angelica and leave Freya alone. If she loses one more hour of sleep because of you, I take something you'll miss." Alphonse continued, his voice laced with command, not suggestion. "I expect her to be at full recovery by Monday. And she will be."

He knew Alphonse wasn't just giving him an order—he was stressing that there would be no second chances.Lucas, still trembling and bloodied, nodded weakly, unable to muster any further response. He stumbled to his feet, his vision still blurry from the pain, and made his way to the door, each step a reminder of the power Alphonse held over him.

Still dazed and bleeding, Lucas staggered out of the hotel, fumbling with trembling hands for his phone. At last, he was able to dial Angelica's number. Her voice, frantic and laden with guilt, answered the phone after just one ring.

"What the *fuck,* Angelica?!" Lucas growled, his voice hoarse from the pain and anger coursing through him.

"I'm sorry, Lucas!" She responded, her voice trembling. "He paid for the room, the car, and the silence. I'm two months behind, Lucas. I chose the rent."

"You could have *warned* me first!" Lucas shouted, his fury bubbling to the surface. His heart raced, and the pounding in his head intensified. The realization of how badly she had set him up made him feel sick.

Angelica paused, her voice less loud but no less urgent. "It's as if you would not have paid attention to what I said. Lucas, you're set in your ways. You would not have heeded my warning, even if I had."

Lucas, hardly able to control his rage, snarled in frustration. "You threw me to the wolves without so much as a heads-up!"

Angelica sighed on the other end of the line, her tone a mix of guilt and defensiveness. "You know how it is, Lucas. I needed the money. You... you should have known Kingsman doesn't play around."

Lucas clenched his fists, his body still trembling from the encounter. He wanted to lash out, to scream, but the truth was, Angelica was right. He'd underestimated the situation. He had walked into it blind, not realizing just how dangerous Alphonse Kingsman truly was.

"You're lucky I'm still standing," Lucas muttered bitterly.

Even though Angelica's voice grew softer, they were now clearly separated. "Lucas, there was nothing I could do. I'm sorry."

Lucas let out a sharp sigh, knowing that there was nothing more to say but still feeling a strong sense of betrayal. He had been played—by Kingsman, by Angelica—and now he had to bear the repercussions.

He said bluntly, "Just... don't call me again," and hung up, feeling as though everything was weighing him down as he stood by himself in the street.

CHAPTER FIFTEEN

Freya walked into the office after a couple of days of much-needed rest, feeling noticeably better. The dull ache in her ribs had subsided, and the sharp discomfort that had once made every movement painful was now just a faint memory. She straightened up as she entered, feeling lighter both physically and mentally.

Lucas hadn't been home over the weekend. She didn't have the energy to deal with another confrontation, another emotional setback. His absence had given her the space she desperately needed to recover—not just physically, but emotionally. It had allowed her to focus solely on herself for once, something she hadn't done in far too long.

The quiet moments alone had helped her recharge, but now, as she stepped back into the office environment, she knew she had to refocus. The looming tasks ahead, especially the ones involving Alphonse, required her to be sharp.

As she reached her desk, she noticed something out of the ordinary—a white box placed carefully on top, with a single white rose resting in the center. Her brows furrowed in confusion, and curiosity tugged at her as she stepped closer.

A small note was attached to the box, the handwriting immediately recognizable. Freya's lips twitched into a smile before she could stop herself. The words were simple but unmistakably Alphonse.

"Better than your dinosaur. -A."

She snorted softly, rolling her eyes as she imagined his smirk while writing the note. Of course, he hadn't forgotten her ancient, bulky laptop. Just as she was tucking the note away, Elihaj strolled by, pausing with a raised eyebrow. "New admirer?" he teased, his tone playful as his eyes flicked between the white rose and her flushed face.

Freya quickly hid the note behind her back as she shook her head. "No, nothing like that," she mumbled, trying to sound casual, though the heat rising in her cheeks betrayed her.

Elihaj grinned, clearly unconvinced, but didn't press further. "Uh-huh, sure," he said, giving her a knowing look before heading back to his desk.

Freya quietly exhaled, relieved that the conversation had ended. She looked back at the white box, her fascination growing once more. Carefully, she opened it, revealing a sleek, top-of-the-line laptop nestled inside.

She chuckled softly, shaking her head. The gesture was a reminder of the control and power he wielded, even in the smallest details of life.

Freya's phone pinged, pulling her attention away from the new laptop. She glanced at the screen and saw a message. The notification included an attachment containing her schedule for the week. As she opened it, a sigh escaped her lips.

Monday, 10:00 AM—Meeting at Kingsman's Office (Review of financial records for potential money laundering)

Wednesday, 1:00 PM—Lunch Meeting at Vero's Bistro (Discuss findings related to suspicious expenses)

Thursday, 3:30 PM—Financial Review at Kingsman's Office (Analysis of flagged expense reports)

Friday, 12:00 PM—Lunch Meeting at The Lexington Hotel (Discuss implications of the investigation and next steps)

Really? As she scrolled through the meticulously laid-out appointments, she wondered to herself. *Who was her boss now—Johnson on paper or Kingsman in practice?*

The answer felt obvious. Despite Johnson still being her official supervisor, Alphonse's influence had grown larger with each passing day. His control wasn't just over the projects she worked on—it was creeping into every aspect of her professional life, right down to her schedule. And the fact that he could make these moves so easily was unsettling.

She put the phone down, rubbing her temples as she stared at the new laptop. There was a part of her that appreciated the gesture, the way Alphonse made sure she had what she needed, but there was another part that felt like she was losing more control of her life with every step he took.

How far would he go?

***

Freya's heels clicked softly on the polished floor as she entered Alphonse's office lobby. This time, there was an uncanny silence—his regular helper Lydia was not present. Freya scowled a little but dismissed it as she made her way to the opulent doors leading to Alphonse's office.

As she reached for the door, it suddenly flew open. Alphonse appeared in the doorway, still engrossed in the documents he held in his hand, his sharp blue eyes scanning the pages. He held the door without looking up—habit, not chivalry—and it still felt like an invitation.

Freya hesitated for a moment before stepping in. The air in his office always felt heavier, filled with a strange mix of tension and power. As she passed him, she felt the door gently close behind her—and then a hand slipped the bag from her shoulder.

She froze, startled by the unexpected gesture. He slid the strap off her shoulder and set the bag by the couch. Her body registered it before her pride did.

She had never seen Alphonse do something like that—so casual. Her heart pounded, unsure whether to feel flustered or irritated by his nonchalance.

Alphonse eventually raised his head from the papers and gave her a slightly amused look. With an expression that was half impatient and half challenging, he stood by the couch with one eyebrow up.

"Are you going to work?" His quiet but subtly commanding tone jolted Freya out of her reverie.

She snapped out of her daze with a blink. Still reeling from the bizarre encounter, she gathered herself and made her way to her spot.

Alphonse went to his desk as Freya sat down, her thoughts still swirling from the previous encounter. She thought he would go back to where he usually was, perhaps by the window or back at his massive desk, but instead he picked up a pile of papers and came over to sit next to her.

Startled, Freya blinked. During their meetings, Alphonse seldom sat this close. He was always in the background, looming over her from across the room and in charge of everything with a detached authority. Now, he stood beside her, effortlessly placing the papers on the coffee table.

Is this really Alphonse Kingsman? she thought, her heart racing slightly.

Before she could process it further, the door opened, and Lydia stepped in carrying a tray of coffee cups and bags from Starbucks. Freya shot Lydia a confused glance, but the assistant just smiled warmly as she placed the coffee and food on the table.

Alphonse replied, his gaze still fixed on the stack of papers, "Thank you, Lydia."

Lydia gave a small nod before slipping out of the room, the door behind her gently closing.

Alphonse pointed to the coffee cups and turned to face Freya. "Coffee," he said matter-of-factly. "Extra shot, no sugar, half-and-half."

Freya's eyes widened as she stared at the cup. It was her usual order. She had a specific preference for her coffee, even down to the smallest detail.

She gaped at him, still trying to reconcile this sudden shift in his behavior. She leaned in to touch his forehead as though she were checking for a fever. "Are you okay, Mr. Kingsman?" she asked.

But with a stern and piercing gaze, He caught her wrist, lowering it with a look. "Miss Blackwood, I'm a gentleman. Unlike others."

She was taken aback by his words, which had a deep yet nuanced meaning that made her heart race. The implication was obvious, and it was impossible to ignore the slight but important change in his manner.

"It's the first time you've greeted me with coffee," Freya remarked, still taken aback by Alphonse's sudden thoughtfulness. She studied him, wondering if this was part of a deeper game he was playing.

Alphonse barely glanced up from the documents, his lips curling into a slight, dismissive smile. "I would have preferred Le Blanc's," he replied smoothly. "But your kind are attached to silly social branding like Starbucks." He said the name with clear disdain, as if the very idea of it offended his sensibilities.

Freya blinked, momentarily stunned. "Kind?" she repeated, her voice tinged with surprise. "Are we a different species now?"

Alphonse set the document aside and fixed his icy gaze on her. "You are a creature of pattern, Miss Blackwood. I prefer patterns I can predict."

Freya gasped, taken aback by the bluntness of his words. "How very unmanly of you, Mr. Kingsman," she shot back, trying to hide her surprise behind a sarcastic irritability.

As he saw her response, Alphonse's eyes lit up with laughter, and a tiny smile formed at the corner of his lips. "Accuracy is not unmanly."

Freya crossed her arms, pretending to be indignant, though she couldn't deny the strange magnetism that came with his provocations. Alphonse's gaze lingered on her for a moment, then he returned to the stack of documents, leaving her to wonder just how deep this game of theirs would go.

CHAPTER SIXTEEN

Freya saw Lucas was back as soon as she entered the house. His usual lack of attention to neatness was evident in the casual way he tossed his jacket over the couch. After everything that had transpired, she was uncertain of what to anticipate and paused for a moment, keeping her hand on the doorknob. Lucas smiled enthusiastically as he came out of their bedroom before she could collect her thoughts.

He exclaimed, "Frey!" with a cheerful tone, as if nothing had happened between them. "How are you feeling?"

Still shocked by his sudden warmth, Freya blinked. Uncertain of the direction of the conversation, she cautiously said, "I'm… okay."

Before she could continue, Lucas gathered her in a bear hug and encircled her with his arms. She was startled by the gesture and tensed up in his arms for a second. She could feel the warmth of his body against hers, but it didn't make the distance between them any less apparent.

"I'm sorry," he said into her hair—too soft, too easy. Promises always came cheap after impact.

Freya said nothing, her thoughts racing. The weight of their recent arguments and the betrayal hung over her desire to believe him. She could feel him trying, but was it enough?

"How about some Korean food you like?" Lucas added, pulling back slightly to look at her with hopeful eyes. "We can order from that place you love."

Freya gave a small nod, forcing a faint smile. "Sure," she replied, but inside, the dissonance between her desired feelings and her actual emotions was growing.

There was also the swelling in Luca's nose that caught her attention. She did try to ask, but Lucas would brush it off. "Pick-up soccer," he said too fast, the lie still wet.

Over the coming days, Lucas appeared resolute in his efforts to improve the situation. He was unusually cheerful, his usual brooding demeanor replaced with an almost exaggerated enthusiasm. He made every effort to simplify her life by tidying up after himself, preparing dinner, and even managing household chores that Freya typically took care of.

There were no awkward confrontations, no tension-filled arguments. Instead, Lucas showered her with affection, but in a way that felt distant. His gestures were kind, but there was no depth behind them. He hugged her often, wrapping her in his arms as if he was afraid of losing her, and when they sat together, he'd kiss the top of her head softly, as if that alone could mend what was broken between them.

But, in spite of his best efforts, there was no sexual approach, no intimacy beyond those fleeting touches. He seemed to understand that striving for more would only lead to distance, so he stayed within the bounds of simple affection, which included whispered assurances, gentle kisses, and light hugs.

Freya was overcome with conflict. A part of her was grateful for his efforts, the calm in their house a sharp contrast to the emotional upheaval of the previous weeks. However, she couldn't get rid of the feeling that something was lacking. His affection felt rehearsed, like he was trying to make up for something, but the connection—the real emotional bond they used to share—felt distant.

She watched him closely during those days, noticing how hard he was trying to please her, yet unsure if his efforts were enough to heal the growing gap between them.

Subtle changes had also occurred at work. During their meetings, Alphonse had become more present, constantly watching her with that unreadable gaze. Their conversations had become more lighthearted, with teasing that veered just shy of being too formal but never descended into anything blatantly improper. They all seemed to be playing a game of concealment, careful not to let the tension escalate.

Freya missed the spark of their past interactions and the heat that once existed between them, but she couldn't deny it in her heart.

It was Friday noon when things shifted.

Freya had rushed that morning, realizing too late that she hadn't washed her usual work clothes. Her pencil skirts—the staple of her professional wardrobe—were all in need of cleaning, forcing her to grab a pair of tailored suit pants she hadn't worn in a while. She barely had time to fix her hair before heading out to her meeting.

When she arrived at the reserved conference room in the hotel, Alphonse was already there, waiting alongside another man. Her heels clicked against the polished floor as she approached, her breath slightly uneven from the hurried morning.

As soon as Alphonse's eyes landed on her, she noticed the subtle flicker of something in his expression—annoyance? His gaze swept over her, taking in the suit pants instead of the skirts she usually wore. Freya's stomach tightened as she caught the brief flash of dissatisfaction before he regained his usual composure.

"This is Ashton Locke," Alphonse said, his voice smooth but with an edge. "My lawyer. He'll be reviewing the documents so far to assess how we can proceed."

Freya nodded politely at Ashton, but her mind was elsewhere, replaying that brief moment of disapproval from Alphonse. It wasn't like him to let his feelings show so easily, but it was clear something about her appearance had irritated him.

Freya tried to concentrate as Ashton started going over the paperwork and talking about the legalities, but her mind kept returning to Alphonse. She sensed his presence next to her, the way his eyes would occasionally rest on her even as the lawyer talked. Something unsaid charged the air between them, making it feel heavier than usual.

Why is my attire so important to him?

"Thank you for your time, Locke," Alphonse said coolly, shaking hands with his lawyer. Ashton Locke gave a brief nod and exited the room. He flipped the privacy latch on his way out. The hallway's red light glowed: do-not-disturb.

Alphonse's hand slammed down on the table just as she was about to get up and grab her folders. Startled, her heart pounding, she glanced up at him. He leaned over her, his intense gaze fixed on hers.

"You changed the uniform." His gaze cut down, then back to her face. "You knew I'd notice."

"I didn't have time to—"

He stepped in. Heat, cologne, the steady line of his breath. "I don't like them on you." he said, his voice low and almost dangerous. "Tell me you'll wear skirts—for me."

She stumbled, her voice faltering under the pressure of his stare. "Pardon me, when did we start having dress codes?"

Alphonse replied, "Always," standing erect now with a composed and cold face. He wasn't kidding; there was a seriousness in his voice, a command that sounded much more intimate than formal.

Freya stood up, squaring her shoulders, and began, trying to maintain a steady voice, "Well, you should—"

But Alphonse moved with quick, purposeful force before she could finish.

Suddenly, with a force that left her gasping for air, he drew her into his arms and closed the distance between them. His mouth slammed down on hers, ferocious and relentless; the kiss was ravenous and devouring.

His hands found her waist, holding her there as if to challenge her to move, and Freya's world whirled as the kiss's intensity overcame her. Instantly, a spark of heat between them ignited and grew into a full-fledged fire.

She gasped against his lips, her hands automatically gripping the front of his shirt for balance. Her thoughts vanished into the swirl of sensation as her heart thumped frantically in her chest.

As though he couldn't get enough, his hand moved up her back to draw her in and press her body against his. Freya melted into him. The intensity of his touch overwhelmed her senses, burning every nerve.

It was raw, unrefined, and powerful. There was no going back now that the dam had broken. His dominance was unmistakable, yet it was thrilling, sending a thrill down her spine as she surrendered to the moment.

She tried to steady herself while they parted just enough for her to gasp for air, with their lips inches from hers. Her body was pressed against his, her hands still gripping the front of his shirt, and there was no mistaking the heat between them.

As he held her, the restraint barely keeping him back, she could feel the tension in his chest and the raggedness of Alphonse's breath. His sharp blue eyes met hers, and Freya felt the full impact of his intensity at that precise moment.

His low, menacing voice sent a chill down her spine as he exhaled, "I'm going to burn those annoying pants off you."

Freya's heart raced at his words, and the force of his voice made her legs weak. The primal intensity of his tone left her breathless with anticipation. Alphonse's hands securely held her waist in place as he raised her onto the conference table. He loomed over her, his presence overwhelming, even though she was seated on the table. He reached up and grabbed her chin, making her look into his eyes. "From now on, only skirts."

His other hand moved down her abdomen and easily slipped into her pants; he leaned in and pressed his hot breath against her ear. Without hesitation, he found her and began to caress her with purposeful, playful strokes. Freya shivered, the heat rising in her, her head tilting back instinctively at the sensation.

"Eyes on me," he growled, his voice cutting through her haze.

Her gaze snapped back to him, locking onto those intense blue eyes as his fingers expertly worked her. She experienced pleasure with each flick of his touch, and she could see the satisfaction in his smirk as he observed her responses. He would watch, relishing the control he had over her body.

"Pants should be illegal," he murmured, thrusting a finger into her. She stifled a gasp, her hips twitching, but he noticed the small reaction and pulled out, only to plunge back in again with a deliberate, steady rhythm.

"Conference room," she warned—half plea, half dare.

"Door's locked," he said, voice low. "Eyes on me."

He didn't even blink, his fingers moving faster and rougher, drawing another soft whimper from her lips. His smirk deepened as he leaned in closer, his breath brushing her cheek. "Skirts," he said, a private rule, not a law. "Ours," he repeated, his lips almost touching hers as she bit down on her own to keep from moaning out loud. "Is that understood?"

Just as she was on the brink, her body trembling with the promise of release, he suddenly stopped. The smirk on his face assured her that he understood exactly what he was doing. She gasped for breath, her pulse pounding in her ears due to the denial of release. "Yes," she finally whispered.

Alphonse slowly pulled his hand from her pants, his fingers glistening with her arousal. With a smug, satisfied look, he raised them to his lips and licked them clean, his eyes locked on hers the whole time.

Her cheeks flushed hard, her body still throbbing with need. He'd never done that before, and it made her even more desperate, the heat spreading under her skin.

Adjusting his suit with calm precision, Alphonse stepped back, his expression as composed as ever. "I'll see you tomorrow."

Freya straightened up, her legs still weak as she tested her footing. "But tomorrow's—"

Alphonse cut her off with a sharp, icy glare. "César will pick you up," he said, his voice cold and final. Then, without another word, he turned and walked out, leaving her flushed, trembling, and craving more.

***

"I don't know what I'm going to do, Sofia," Freya muttered, frowning as she lifted a spoonful of ice cream to her lips.

They were lounging in her living room, both dressed in cozy pajamas, with Netflix playing in the background. But their attention wasn't on the show.

"He's… a lot," Freya said. "And I don't want to say no." Freya admitted, her voice tinged with frustration.

Sofia looked over at her, raising an eyebrow. "This is a first coming from a woman who's always been so self-sufficient."

Freya sighed, sinking deeper into the couch. "I didn't know I could enjoy sex like that. It's dangerous, Sofia. Like, I thought I had control, but with him, it's…different."

Sofia laughed, nudging Freya's shoulder playfully. "Well, there's always a first for everything, babe. Every man is different, and clearly, Alphonse knows what he's doing."

Freya nodded, still swirling the spoon in her half-melted ice cream. "I keep choosing him. That's the part that scares me."

Sofia's expression softened. "And Lucas? How's that mess going?"

Freya paused, her gaze drifting off for a moment. "He's been different," she said quietly, setting the spoon back in the bowl. "Not just different because of the cheating, but more… submissive. He's been trying hard to make me happy, but now everything he does feels like it has double meanings. Like he's compensating for something or trying to manipulate me into forgetting what he did."

Sofia hummed in understanding. "Maybe he's realizing he messed up and is trying to get back in your favorable graces. But let me guess, it's not working?"

Freya shook her head. "No, it's not. Everything feels hollow now. I see him trying, but I can't shake the feeling that I don't care as much anymore. And with Alphonse…" She trailed off, biting her lip.

Sofia gave her a knowing look. "You're falling for Alphonse, aren't you?"

Freya exhaled, closing her eyes briefly. "I don't know if it's falling. But I'm definitely something. He challenges me and makes me feel things I've never felt before. With Lucas, everything just feels... bland."

Sofia smirked. "Sounds like you've got a lot to figure out, girl. However, based on your description, Lucas seems to be well-established. What about Alphonse? Indeed, I advise you to relish the journey, yet exercise prudence.

Even though Freya laughed quietly, the situation's gravity persisted. Even though she knew she had decisions to make, everything with Alphonse felt so out of her control—dangerous and exciting at the same time.

"Too bad Layla isn't here," Freya sighed, leaning back against the couch.

Sofia erupted in laughter. "She would've made you call Lucas right now to dump him and then ordered Alphonse over to, well, you know, fuck you senseless."

They both laughed, the sound filling the room, and for a moment, Freya felt lighter. Layla's approach of pushing Freya to confront things directly was quite typical.

"But seriously, Freya," Sofia said, her laughter fading into a more serious tone. "Why do you still keep up with Lucas? It's clear things aren't the same. There's no sexual exchange, no real connection anymore. Why keep it up?"

Freya frowned, dropping her spoon into the pint of ice cream. She stared at the melting mess, her thoughts drifting. "I guess I'm scared to let go of what I've known," she admitted quietly, her voice laced with vulnerability. "Sofia, we've been together for years. He seemed like the one for me. Letting go of that makes me feel as though I'm giving up on something I had assumed would last forever."

Reaching out, Sofia put a reassuring hand on Freya's knee. "I understand. It feels like a failure to leave a relationship you've spent so much time in. However, based on what you've told me, Freya, it seems to be over already. It is merely the specter of its former self."

Freya nodded, fighting back tears as her throat constricted. "I am aware. I simply... I thought I knew. And now it feels like nothing is certain."

A tiny smile came to Sofia's face. "Although uncertainty can be frightening, it can also indicate that it might be time to try something different. Because of the past, you don't have to hold on to Lucas. You are worthy of better—someone who challenges and thrills you."

With her fears weighing heavily on her, Freya inhaled deeply. "Perhaps you are correct. I simply feel afraid."

Sofia gave her knee a squeeze. "Freya, you underestimate your strength. You'll figure it out. If Alphonse is involved in your quest for discovery, then relish the journey. But don't let fear hold you back from what could be so much better than what you've known."

Freya smiled faintly, knowing Sofia was right. But even with that knowledge, letting go was never easy.

CHAPTER SEVENTEEN

Freya sat stiffly in the back of the sleek black SUV, staring out the window as the familiar streets passed by. It was a quiet Saturday noon, and usually, she'd be working from home, buried in her reports and documents. But not today.

Because of Alphonse Kingsman.

Nobody says no to Kingsman.

She snorted to herself at the thought. I should start saying no, she mused, imagining how that would rattle his perfect little ego. The idea amused her briefly before she shifted her focus back to the situation at hand.

After their heated conversation the previous Friday, Freya knew better than to even glance at her collection of pants this morning. Instead, she had chosen a blue halter dress, simple but elegant, the kind that clung just enough to make her feel confident but still allowed her to feel professional. Her hair hung loosely down her back, providing some cover for the bare skin the dress left exposed.

The SUV pulled up to an elegant shopping mall, the kind of place where high-end brands ruled and price tags were better left unseen. The name of the mall, Luxe Galerie, stood tall in gold letters—a place Layla adored but one Freya rarely indulged in. She'd once saved for three weeks just to buy a single dress here, surviving on ramen noodles to afford it. Now, she was being dropped off like royalty.

As the door opened, César, Alphonse's ever-loyal and warm driver, greeted her with a smile. He was large and imposing, dressed in his usual black suit, with a discreet earpiece tucked in his ear. He gestured for her to follow a sharply dressed woman waiting near the valet.

"Miss Blackwood," the woman greeted her, a touch of nervousness in her smile. "Please, follow me."

They walked into the mall, the air-conditioned luxury immediately engulfing them. Freya could feel eyes on them, curious glances thrown her way as César followed like a bodyguard. Fucking Kingsman territory, she thought, rolling her eyes internally. I'm going to slap him for making me go through this.

They entered an elegant store lined with exquisite clothing, the kind that screamed opulence. Freya could already hear Layla squealing in her mind, ogling the high-end fashion pieces on display. She was confident that her friend would experience immense joy in such a setting.

The woman led them to a private room in the back. It was secluded, undoubtedly a place where people like Alphonse tried on clothes without being bothered by the common folk. The room was tastefully decorated with plush couches and a selection of refreshments on the side. Designer clothes were carefully displayed, and two store employees stood nearby, waiting. There were no cameras here.

But her eyes were immediately drawn to Alphonse. He was sitting on the couch, dressed casually but still managing to look effortlessly elegant. Of course, he was drinking. He sipped more than he drank; control was his only real intoxication

His gaze landed on her, and a familiar smirk tugged at the corner of his lips.

"Ah, Miss Blackwood," he greeted smoothly.

He set his drink down on the coffee table and rose from the couch with his usual graceful confidence, walking over to her. His hand brushed over her bare shoulder as he gestured to the employee standing nearby. "Bring over the selection," he instructed, his tone cool and commanding.

Freya's eyes flicked to the mirror in front of the couch as Alphonse guided her toward it, his hands resting possessively on her shoulders. She could see the controlled expression on his face, the way his eyes studied her through the reflection. "Since we'll be dealing with legal matters," he began, his voice icy, "I need you to be presentable under such circumstances."

The employee entered again, carrying several garments, all with skirts. *You really hated those pants, bastard,* Freya thought bitterly, her lips pressing into a thin line.

"You want to doll me up?" She asked, raising an eyebrow at him.

Alphonse leaned closer, his breath brushing the back of her neck. His grin was infuriatingly confident. "I'm going to enjoy this," he said, his voice sending a shiver down her spine.

Straightening up, he glanced at the employees. "Leave those here and all of you out." His voice was sharp, dismissing them with a single command.

The staff bowed quickly, filing out of the room along with César, leaving the two of them alone. The door clicked shut behind them. Alphonse strode over to the display of clothes, carefully selecting one of the outfits before walking back to Freya. He handed it to her, and her eyes immediately caught the price tag. She gasped, wide-eyed.

"This is too much!" she exclaimed, holding the outfit like it might burn her fingers.

Alphonse chuckled, the sound low and amused. "It's irrelevant now."

"I can't wear something this expensive," she protested, glancing at the delicate fabric.

His gaze hardened, his tone leaving no room for argument. "Put it on."

Freya sighed in frustration, knowing there was no point in arguing with him. She turned with the intention of heading to the dressing room at the back, but Alphonse's voice abruptly stopped her.

"Right here."

She spun around, her eyes widening in surprise. "Excuse me?"

He stood there, hands in his pockets, his smirk never fading. "Here," he repeated, his tone firm, his eyes glinting with amusement. It was clear now—this was what he meant when he said he'd enjoy it. He wanted her to strip right in front of him, knowing full well she was at his mercy.

Freya's heart pounded in her chest, a mix of anger and adrenaline. *Damn him.* He was enjoying every moment of this power play. Why am I excited?

Her eyes, defiant and fiery, only widened Alphonse's smirk. He tapped his foot against the floor, waiting, teasing. "Well," he began, voice dripping with amusement, "do you need me to—"

"I'm fine!" Freya snapped, moving back slightly, avoiding his attempt to grab her. She saw a flicker of enjoyment in his eyes, the satisfaction that came from her resistance.

He walked to the couch with an effortless grace, never taking his eyes off her. Sitting down in the middle, he positioned himself so that he could watch her reflection in the mirror. "Proceed."

Freya's expression was fuming, but she followed through, her fingers slowly loosening the halter of her dress. The fabric slipped down her body, revealing her in nothing but her underwear. Every move was deliberate and slow, but she never lost that determined fire in her gaze as she undressed in front of him, eyes locking with his in the mirror.

He was enjoying every second, and she could tell by the hunger in his eyes and the way he remembered her nude skin. She should have retaliated, but she felt so exhilarated by his stare that she didn't want to stop.

Once she had finished slipping into the first outfit, he rose from the couch. His hands found her waist, sliding down to her ass, where the skirt clung to her perfectly. His fingers traced the hem at her thighs, the heat of his touch making her shiver. "I like it," he said, his voice a low rumble, settling the fabric.

His hand moved to her chin, tilting her face up so their eyes met directly, no mirror between them. "Do you like it?"

Her gaze flicked over him briefly before she gave a nod. "It's still expensive for my taste."

He chuckled, a rich, smooth sound. "You look better wrapped in something with a hefty price tag."

Freya's lips curled slightly. "How much do I have to work to earn it, Mr. Kingsman?"

His lips hovered dangerously close to hers, a sly grin playing on his face. "Hmm," he hummed, the vibration of his voice sending a shiver through her. "Why don't you try the other one?"

"What if I don't?"

Before Alphonse could respond, she rose up on her toes, her lips catching his lower one, biting down softly before pulling back, her retreat quick and teasing. It caught him completely by surprise, and before he could grab her, she was already walking toward the next outfit.

In one swift stride, he was behind her, his hand grasping her arm and spinning her around. His imposing figure loomed over her as he pushed her back against the wall. Freya gasped, but her cry vanished as Alphonse's lips crashed against hers, devouring her with a kiss that was strong, fierce, and filled with desire.

His hands found her ass, lifting her easily as her legs wrapped around his waist. He deepened the kiss with a low growl, the tension between them burning hotter than ever, as if the fight in her only made him want her more.

"Is everything okay?" A voice called from the doorway, and the door creaked open, revealing a concerned employee.

Alphonse broke the kiss, his face darkening with fury, anger radiating off him in waves. Freya hastily untangled herself from his grip, straightening her clothes and spinning around, her heart pounding in her chest.

"Everything's fine!" she blurted, cutting off Alphonse before he could unleash his temper. Her eyes flicked to the employee, silently pleading for them to leave, as she caught sight of the murderous look darkening Alphonse's expression.

The door slammed shut abruptly, with the employee clearly sensing the tension.

Alphonse was already moving toward the door, a predator on the hunt, his entire demeanor rigid with simmering rage. Freya's heart leaped into her throat—if she didn't stop him, that poor employee would face the brunt of it. Acting fast, she grabbed his arm, and she pulled him back with all her strength, crashing her lips against his in a desperate attempt to redirect his focus.

At first, his body was still tense, the anger not fully gone. But as her lips pressed insistently against his, her tongue slipping between his lips, she felt him soften. His rigid posture eased as the kiss deepened, the intensity shifting from fury to heat. Alphonse's hands found her waist again, gripping her tightly, and soon the kiss became hungry, a slow burn turning into fire.

Freya broke away, breathless. "If we keep going, I'll ruin this outfit before I even get a chance to wear it."

Alphonse exhaled, still close, his forehead brushing hers. "I'll buy another one. I don't care."

She let out a playful laugh, slapping his chest lightly. "Don't be so careless. How are you going to explain that on your expense report?"

That earned a chuckle from him, the tension finally dissipating. "Do you think this was just to doll you up?" he muttered, his eyes gleaming with a mix of amusement and desire.

Alphonse turned her suddenly, pinning Freya against the wall with deliberate force. The unmistakable press of his arousal against her lower back left her breathless.

His lips grazed the shell of her ear, breath hot and teasing.

Then his left hand slid down, tracing the outside of her thigh, slow and possessive. Freya's spine arched when his palm moved up—over the curve of her ass—while his fingertips slipped beneath the fabric of her underwear, trailing toward the heat between her legs.

She gasped.

"Are you aware of how delicious your responses are?" He whispered, his voice low at her ear. "How much does your body want me?"

His fingers found her center, slipping between the slick folds, and she instinctively tensed—eyes fluttering shut as she fought to keep quiet.

"How wet you get when I touch you…" he murmured.

"Alphonse—" she breathed, her voice tinged with panic. Anyone could walk in.

But Alphonse didn't move. Didn't hesitate. Didn't care.

His mouth dropped to her nape, lips parting just enough to suck, teeth grazing her skin. Freya's knees trembled as his finger pressed and circled over her clit with slow, devastating intent.

"How you moan for me," he said, and she could hear the smirk in his voice.

"We're in a—ah—" she tried again, struggling to speak through the wave of sensation.

But he cut her off with a slow stroke that forced a moan from her lips—soft, involuntary, helpless.

"See?" he growled, lips brushing her ear again. "Only I can make you feel like this."

And God, he wasn't wrong.

Lucas had never come close.

Freya's hands braced against the wall, her breath hot against the painted surface. Her pulse thundered in her ears as Alphonse pressed his body tighter against hers, the rigid heat of his arousal grinding into her lower back.

"You like this," he whispered, his voice dark silk. "Being touched here... where anyone could walk in and see how ruined I make you."

They moved with expert rhythm, stroking between her folds, finding her clit, and coaxing soft, breathy sounds from her throat. The lace of her underwear was damp now.

"You should hear yourself," he murmured, his free hand sliding up her side, curling possessively around her waist. "Every breath. Every whimper. It's all mine."

"Alphonse..." She gasped again, a shaky attempt at restraint. "Please—"

He turned her chin toward him, just enough for her to see the hunger in his eyes.

"Begging already?"

He didn't wait for a reply.

His hand left her briefly—just long enough to tug her panties down to mid-thigh, and then his fingers were back, sliding into her wet heat with a force that made her bite her lip to stifle a moan.

"God, look at you," he groaned against her shoulder. "So fucking tight. Always ready for me."

Freya pressed her head to the wall, her body arching into his touch despite herself. She could feel the deep ache building, her body clenching around his fingers as the pressure mounted.

"Say it," he growled into her ear. "Tell me who makes you feel like this."

Her pride held for a second.

Then another slow curl of his fingers, and she shattered.

"You," she gasped. "Only you."

***

Alphonse sat back comfortably in his chair, his posture relaxed, one hand swirling a glass of whiskey as he watched her with an amused expression. He seemed almost too calm, as if he had carefully curated every detail of the evening. Alphonse had, without much conversation, pulled them to the upper terrace of a fancy restaurant there, and it was immediately apparent that he was a regular. Employees gave him respectful greetings, and even the chef came out of the kitchen to shake his hand.

Freya couldn't help but take in the beauty of the place—the elegant décor, the view of the cityscape, and the scent of gourmet dishes filling the air. It was the kind of restaurant she might have dreamt of visiting, but definitely not on a Saturday like this. Despite herself, she was impressed.

"How much alcohol do you need to continue our encounter?" he asked, his voice low and teasing.

Freya snorted, barely stopping herself from spilling the drink she was sipping. She shot him a playful glare. "You think I need alcohol to manage you, Mr. Kingsman?"

Alphonse's smirk deepened. "You were pretty wild that first night."

Her cheeks flushed at the memory, and she quickly looked away, trying to play it off. "I thought it was going to be a one-night thing," she muttered, taking another sip of her drink.

Alphonse leaned forward slightly, his eyes glinting with that familiar intensity. "Can we pretend it's a one-night thing every night?"

Freya gaped at him, taken aback by his words. Her eyes flicked to his, searching for a trace of sarcasm or teasing, but all she saw was the same confident, smug expression he always wore. "You're unbelievable," she said, shaking her head.

Alphonse shrugged casually, sipping his drink as if her reaction amused him. "And yet, here you are," he replied smoothly, his smirk never leaving his face.

Freya rolled her eyes, attempting to ignore his words, but she knew he was correct. There was something about him that kept pulling her back, even when she told herself she shouldn't be here. He had a knack for evoking strong emotions in her and adeptly crafted his words to deceive her. And despite how infuriating it was, part of her couldn't help but be drawn in.

Dinner had been quiet, though Alphonse had drunk a considerable amount, gesturing for Freya to join him. By the time they finished, César was already waiting outside, standing stoically in front of the SUV. Despite reeking of alcohol, Alphonse remained as composed as ever, guiding her to the car with his firm grip, opening the door for her, then sliding in beside her. The moment the door closed, his hand immediately pulled her closer, his breath warm against her neck as she found herself half-seated on his lap.

The scent of him was intoxicating—a mix of his cologne and the alcohol he had consumed. Freya couldn't help but wonder if Alphonse ever truly got drunk, his control still unwavering. As he sighed, his hand gently caressed her thigh, causing her pulse to race. She wasn't sure if it was the alcohol or just the pull of the moment, but she found herself leaning into him, her body responding to the heat between them.

Their lips met, and Freya felt like she might melt under the intensity of his kiss. It was breathless—tender, yet charged with hunger. She tilted her head back, permitting him to deepen it, his hand sliding from her neck, down over her breast, and gripping her waist. The soft sound of their lips and the way his touch explored her made everything else fade away.

Her hands moved on their own, sliding around his neck, feeling the tension in his muscles, the rumble of a satisfied growl from his chest. She moved lower, tracing his chest until her fingers found the unmistakable bulge straining against his pants.

Freya shifted slightly, her body twisting as her left hand stayed on his neck, while her right hand fumbled with his belt, unbuttoning his pants with deliberate care. She slipped her hand inside, feeling him hard and ready beneath her touch. Alphonse groaned, a deep sound of approval, his hand tightening its grip on her waist as his hips subtly pressed into her hand.

She hadn't crossed this line with him before. Was it the alcohol making this easier, or was it simply the moment they'd been building toward? Alphonse wasn't stopping her—if he wanted to, he would have by now. The thought thrilled her. He wanted this just as much as she did.

Breaking the kiss, she held his gaze, her hand wrapping around his manhood. His eyes stayed locked on hers, unwavering, filled with that same dark desire.

Will he yield?

Her hand moved slowly, causing his cock to pulse in response. Freya could sense the battle raging within him, the ironclad control he always maintained slipping. His body stiffened, every muscle taut as if he were holding himself back from moving, from giving in completely to the pleasure she was delivering.

His face was buried in her neck, and his teeth grazed her skin. Then his voice broke the silence, with a low tremor to it. "Stop." He placed his hand on her wrist and pulled her hand away. He moved away from the nook of her neck, and their eyes met for a brief moment.

"We're here."

Freya blinked, glancing out the window. They were parked in front of her house. The street was dark, and Lucas's car wasn't there.

Alphonse had already tucked himself away, adjusting his clothes with the same smooth precision he always carried, now back in control, his usual composed self. He stepped out of the car first, opening her door and offering his hand. Her clothes were still wrinkled, a telltale sign of their encounter, but as she stepped out, Alphonse reached for her, straightening her dress and smoothing out her hair, his touch surprisingly tender after the heated moment they shared.

He didn't say a word, but there was something in his eyes—something possessive, something that told her the encounter wasn't over. He walked her to the door, his presence steady beside her, leaving the quiet tension between them to linger, heavy and unspoken.

Freya barely had time to register the click of the lock before Alphonse's broad frame pushed her back into the house, closing the door with a quiet thud. Her breath hitched in surprise, confusion flashing across her face as he grabbed her waist, guiding her toward the couch with firm, deliberate steps.

"Alphonse, what—"

His fingers silenced her words, his smirk deepening as her wide-eyed expression lingered. She thought, panic mingling with the intensity of the moment, *This is Lucas's and my house. What is he doing?*

"Now, Miss Blackwood," he began with a smooth and teasing voice, "tell me how many times you have come on this couch?"

Freya blinked, her pulse racing as she shook her head. Alphonse raised an eyebrow, amused. "Not even once?" His lips formed a smug smile as he made fun of her. In his darkly satisfied voice, he remarked, "What a dull boyfriend you have." Don't worry, however. I will take care of that.

His hand moved up her dress, fingers hooking around her underwear and pulling them down in one swift motion. "Don't you dare!" she gasped, but it was too late—he had already pocketed them, his smirk growing more devilish.

"I should also make underwear illegal," he muttered. Before she could reply, Alphonse leaned down, and to her shock, his tongue flicked against her clit.

Freya's body jolted, a sharp gasp escaping her lips as her head fell back, her back arching off the couch. Oh my god. Alphonse wasn't just teasing her—he was devouring her, his mouth working her in ways that left her breathless. The soft, wet strokes of his tongue moved with precision, as if he knew every sensitive spot, every place that made her shiver. Her moans filled the room, her fingers gripping his sleek black hair, tugging as she lost herself in the sensation.

"God, Alphonse," Freya moaned, her voice breaking, "God…"

Her climax was building fast, the pressure inside her rising with every flick of his tongue. As if he sensed that she was nearing her climax, Alphonse slipped his fingers inside her, twisting them just right while his tongue circled her clit with unrelenting skill. "Come for me," he growled, his voice dark and commanding.

Freya's body shattered around him, her orgasm crashing over her as she cried out his name. Her legs trembled, her back arched, and her moans echoed in the quiet room. Alphonse pulled back, smirking as he licked his fingers, satisfied. "One," he said, his tone playful and full of promise.

Before she could catch her breath, he leaned in, his eyes gleaming with lust. "Now," he murmured, his grin wicked, "let's go for two."

***

After Freya's second orgasm, Alphonse lifted her effortlessly, ignoring her half-hearted protests. "Alphonse, we shouldn't—" she managed to say, but he wasn't taking no for an answer. His grip was firm, and she wrapped her legs around his waist instinctively, her body already surrendering to him.

Within seconds, they were in the bedroom she shared with Lucas. The bed she'd spent countless nights in with him now felt foreign as Alphonse threw her down onto it, his broad frame blocking the door with a quiet click as it shut behind him.

"Should we make it the third right here on the bed?" He teased, his voice full of dark amusement.

Freya's heart pounded as she lay there, her body trembling not with fear, but with anticipation. This was Lucas's bed, *their* bed. Her mind flickered to the nights he stayed out late, the excuses, and the lies. "He cheated on you," a voice in her head reminded her. Had he done it here, on this bed?

Alphonse hovered over her, his presence overwhelming, and his hand slid down her body as if it claimed every inch of her. "Shall I show you what a real man is?" he asked, his fingers spreading her legs and quickly finding her soaked core. She moaned uncontrollably, her body betraying her better judgment as pleasure flooded through her.

But fear nagged her senses—what if Lucas returned home? What if he walked in and discovered her with another man? Alphonse's fingers kept sliding in and out of her, the wet sound of her arousal echoing throughout the room, distracting her from her panic.

He fucking cheated on you. The voice in her head screamed louder. *Had he cared for your feelings when he fucked someone else?*

Alphonse's breath was hot against her neck as he growled in satisfaction, "Hmm, you're ready for me." His fingers slid out, followed by the full, thick presence of his cock. Alphonse moved with a deliberate and exact rhythm, leaving her gasping for breath. Their bodies slammed together with each thrust as he knelt on the bed, lifting her hips while she arched her back. Everything about him exuded raw, controlled dominance: his muscles rippling as he worked in and out of her, the slap of skin, and the low growl of pleasure.

She could feel another orgasm brewing, ready to overpower her, when the unmistakable sound of a car pulling up outside sent a jolt of terror through her.

Shit! Lucas!

Alphonse paused briefly, his lips curving into a smug smirk. He grabbed her by the waist, effortlessly lifting her from the bed and pinning her to the door. She yelped, barely able to contain her shock and pleasure as he thrust into her unrelentingly.

"Freya, are you home?" Lucas's voice called from the hallway. Panic surged through her, but Alphonse did not stop.If anything, the thought of Lucas right outside the door seemed to excite him. "Your boyfriend is calling," he whispered into her ear. "Aren't you going to welcome him home?"

She tried to respond, to form words, but Alphonse slammed into her fiercely, and her cry came out broken, almost like a sob. "Frey, are you okay?" Lucas's voice was closer now, right outside the door.

"I'm fine!" Freya gasped, struggling to steady her voice as Alphonse's cock hit her G-spot with precision, her body betraying her once again. " Exhausted," she stammered, biting her lip to stop herself from moaning.

Alphonse pulled back slightly, watching her with that infuriating smirk. His hand moved to her mouth, tracing her lips with his thumb as he leaned in. "Let me—" Lucas began, the doorknob turning.

"NO!" Freya practically screamed, panic flashing in her eyes. "Shower! Hungry!" She needed him to go now.

There was a pause. "Okay... I'll go out and get you something. Denny's?"

"Yes!" she blurted, barely holding herself together as Alphonse continued to thrust into her, slowly and teasingly, making her body tremble.

The sound of Lucas's car engine starting up and driving away was the only signal she needed, the last thread of tension snapping. Alphonse grinned, his lips brushing her ear as he whispered, "You have no idea how wet you are. How tight you get." His breath was ragged now, his control starting to slip. "Makes me want to come inside you so fucking bad."

"You—" Alphonse's pace quickened, his thrusts becoming harder and deeper, drowning Freya's voice in raw pleasure. The sound of their skin slapping filled the room, the intensity of it making her head spin.

And then it hit her, hard—her body clenched tight around him, a sharp cry escaping her lips as her orgasm tore through her, her nails digging into his shoulders.

Alphonse groaned, deep and guttural, as he buried himself inside her, his release crashing over him, his body shuddering as he spilled into her.

They stayed like that for a moment, both panting, their bodies still intertwined. Freya's mind spun, overwhelmed, as the reality of what had just happened began to settle in.

Alphonse's breath was hot against her ear as he pulled back slightly, still holding her close. "Three," he whispered, a smug grin curling his lips.

CHAPTER EIGHTEEN

Freya stood in her bedroom, fuming as she replayed the events of the previous night over and over in her mind. She had let Alphonse take control, let him push every boundary she had built between them. The audacity of it—the nerve he had to fuck her in the very room she shared with Lucas, with the door inches away from where her boyfriend could have walked in at any moment. Her skin prickled with anger at the memory of that moment, and the worst part was that she had allowed it to happen. She gave it away. That was the problem—she'd liked it.

Her fists clenched at her sides, her mind racing. He had taken liberties no one else would dare, using her vulnerability and her conflicted emotions to bend her to his will. Alphonse Kingsman was always in control and consistently got exactly what he wanted, whenever he wanted it.

Well, not today.

Her eyes darted to the wardrobe standing in the corner of the room. She was determined to exact revenge on him. *Oh, he thinks he's untouchable, does he?* Freya's heart pounded with a thrill that rivaled her anger. She knew how to annoy him—knew exactly how. The goal was to make him lose his composure, at least temporarily. And it was going to start with something as simple as the right pair of pants.

She yanked open the wardrobe doors, her fingers skimming through the hangers until she found them—a pair of sleek, tailored black trousers. They were the epitome of professional chic, and she knew exactly what kind of reaction they'd get from Alphonse. The man had made it painfully clear he didn't want her in pants. He preferred her in skirts, dresses, and anything else that fed his need for dominance and control. However, these pants? She rebelled silently with these.

Slipping into them, Freya smoothed down the fabric as she looked in the mirror. The black pants were perfectly tailored and hugged her figure in all the right places, and the white blouse was tucked in neatly. The entire ensemble was spotless. She accessorized the ensemble with a light scarf draped over her shoulders and polished loafers. Her ensemble was effortless, elegant, and defiant.

She took a deep breath, her mind racing with the possible outcomes of this little act of defiance. There were two possible outcomes. Option one: Alphonse would be irritated all day, glaring at her with his cold, steely gaze, but he would ultimately overlook it. Option two: He would drag her into the nearest private room, rip the pants off her, and punish her in ways she wouldn't be able to resist.

Her heart raced at the thought of option two, the possibility sending a shiver down her spine. But the thought of Alphonse losing his calm, letting his control slip even for a moment, sent a thrill through her.

She knew the risks. Alphonse wasn't a man who enjoyed being challenged. But Freya wasn't someone to back down easily. She had been pushed, too. Alphonse Kingsman had not been annoyed before, but that was only because he had never encountered Freya Blackwood at her most stubborn.

Let him be annoyed, she thought with satisfaction as she gathered her things. Let him try to regain control.

She glanced one last time in the mirror before heading out. Today, she was prepared to engage with him according to her own terms. If he wanted a challenge, she was going to give him one.

She had learned that Alphonse Kingsman didn't understand what it meant to be out of control.

But he was about to find out.

Alphonse sat in his office, trying to drown out the usual chaos of his Monday morning. His phone buzzed relentlessly, his inbox overflowing, but it was the annoying early morning calls that grated on him the most. Still, he found a strange sense of anticipation fueling his focus, something that kept his day tolerable amidst the noise.

Freddy, one of the project managers for a multimillion-dollar development they were working on, had been on the line for what felt like an eternity, droning on about some unforeseen complication. Half-listening, Alphonse's focus was split between the conversation and the restless tug at the back of his mind.

And then his office door opened.

A moment of disbelief flashed across Alphonse's face as he looked up and saw Freya.

What the fuck is she wearing?

Freya stood in the doorway, composed and confident, her outfit both sleek and undeniably provocative in its subtle defiance. She wore perfectly tailored black pants, sharp and professional, hugging her form in a way that made it impossible to ignore. A soft gray scarf draped loosely over her shoulders added a final touch of subtle elegance, and a crisp white blouse with rolled-up sleeves gave her a relaxed, easygoing vibe. Simple, clean, yet defiant, the ensemble was finished with polished loafers and a slim black belt that tightened her waist.

Alphonse's eyes narrowed as they locked onto hers. Her lips curled into a small, teasing grin, the glint in her eyes unmistakable. She knew exactly what she was doing.

She's fucking doing this on purpose.

"Mr. Kingsman?" Freddy's voice crackled through the phone, his tone oblivious to the silent tension now flooding the room.

Alphonse tore his gaze away from Freya, his jaw tightening as frustration simmered beneath the surface. "Get it done," he growled into the phone, his voice sharp and final. Without waiting for a reply, he hung up and slammed the phone down onto the table with a force that echoed through the room.

Freya didn't flinch. She stepped forward, her grin still in place, as if she'd won some small battle. "Good morning, Mr. Kingsman," she said, her tone light but dripping with subtle challenge. "Shall we start?"

Alphonse's eyes flickered over her, the tension in his body palpable. His lips twitched, resisting the urge to snarl. He had made his expectations known, and yet here she was, standing before him in defiance, dressed in a way that both empowered her and taunted him.

She wasn't just dressed for work—she was dressed to *challenge* him. And she knew exactly what she was doing.

She's playing with fire. Alphonse thought, his eyes narrowing as they scanned her from head to toe. Her amused expression and the way she held herself with newfound confidence suggested that she was testing the boundaries, seeing how far she could push before he snapped. That grin infuriated Alphonse as much as it excited him, with the way it tugged at the corner of her lips, daring him to react.

But what she seemed to forget—or perhaps, underestimate—was that Alphonse Kingsman never lost.

He leaned back in his chair, the movement deliberate and slow, as if to show her that he was in control. The silence between them grew thicker by the moment as he folded his hands in his lap and kept his eyes fixed on her. He intended the silence to make her uncomfortable and question her actions, but she stood there, unflinching, waiting. Instead, he let the tension build, his eyes dark with intent, his mind already calculating the next move.

"You think you've won something, Miss Blackwood?" He finally said, his voice low and deliberate, a dangerous edge beneath the calm. "You're playing a dangerous game."

Freya's grin widened slightly, her eyes gleaming with a thrill she didn't bother to hide. She was enjoying this—enjoying pushing him, testing his limits. Her silence was telling, though. She wasn't backing down. She was waiting for his move, daring him to play along.

His lips curled into a slow, predatory smile. "But I should remind you," he continued, his voice soft but chilling, "I always win."

She had sparked the fire between them, but Alphonse was about to fan it into an inferno. Freya thought she knew the game she was playing, but what she didn't realize was that Alphonse controlled the board, the pieces, and the outcome.

She was playing with fire.

But so was he.

***

Alphonse ran a hand through his hair, rough and impatient, his fingers tightening at the base of his skull. The laptop screen before him glowed with lines of untouched data—contracts, budgets, and updates from Milan. Numbers that once commanded his full attention now blurred uselessly before his eyes.

He couldn't focus.

She had burrowed into the quiet spaces of his mind and refused to leave. Every breath he drew felt laced with her—her perfume, the sound of her voice, and the way her laugh curled around him like smoke. It was infuriating. Unreasonable. Unacceptable.

He had expected her to be a one-night distraction. She fulfilled a need that he had previously ignored. He'd told himself that the first night. But when she lay tangled in his sheets, eyes half-lidded, hair a wild halo on his pillow, and a faint, satisfied smile on her lips like she knew something he didn't.

And maybe she had.

Here he was, weeks later, still captivated by her.

Out of pure annoyance—*no, curiosity*, he told himself—he'd looked into her. Expecting what he always found: a lovely face with just enough credentials to get past reception. But instead...

Flawless performance reviews. Project leadership. Clean audits. Departmental efficiency has doubled since her arrival.

Freya Blackwood wasn't a reckless woman.

She was disciplined. Respected.

Exceptional.

That night's events only intensified the frustration. Women like her didn't throw themselves into a stranger's lap. They held on tightly. They didn't look up at him with those soft brown eyes like they meant it when they said, *"I want this."*

But she had.

And worse—*he believed her.*

There was no calculation in her touch. There was no hint of practiced seduction. She hadn't faked a single gasp.

It had been real.

And Alphonse Kingsman, master of control, felt like a man getting drunk on honesty for the first time.

So what the fuck was she doing going back to him?

The memory of her kissing her boyfriend Lucas the night he returned from his business trip etched itself deeply in his mind. Smiling politely. Looking safe. Normal.

It caused a chilling sensation in his chest.

Am I second choice? Was it a mistake she now regrets?

He slammed the laptop shut and stood so fast his chair skidded back, hitting the wall with a dull *thud.*

He couldn't sit still. Pacing, hand dragging down his face. He tried to go back to what he knew: women with boundaries he could buy. He was able to schedule his desires accordingly. Sex is like business: clean and easy.

But Freya wasn't clean or easy.

She was chaos.

She embodied a gentle rebellion, dressed in a pencil skirt. She was the first woman who wanted him for who he was, not his wealth or power.

And he hated her for it. No—he wanted her for it.

That's why he'd pulled strings. That's why he'd hired her firm. That's why he'd asked for their best senior analyst, knowing damn well they'd assign Freya.

He told himself it was a strategy. Business.

But it was an *obsession*. Dressed up in a suit and justification. And now, every time she walked into his office, it was like tearing a seam he hadn't realized was still holding him together.

The tight pants were a constant source of discomfort. She caught his attention with a small smirk. The curve of her mouth when she said "Sir" was just slightly too slow.

She's doing it on purpose, he thought bitterly.

And it's working. His cock stirred behind his zipper. He ground his teeth.

"Fuck."

He pulled off his suit jacket. Threw it across the couch. The tie followed—ripped off with one jerk and flung aside. His pulse thundered in his ears. His control slipped with every second she lived in his mind.

Enough.

No more staring at walls. No more wondering if he mattered to her like she suddenly mattered to him.

He grabbed his keys. He quietly exited the office.

The elevator down felt like it crawled through molasses.

His reflection in the doors showed him a man on the edge—tie loose, eyes dark, lips pressed in a flat, furious line.

The night she danced so close to me, she risked everything.

He was going to knock on her door. He was going to look her in the eye and take back the control she thought she'd stolen.

And he was going to remind her—Alphonse Kingsman doesn't break.

***

Freya tugged at the hem of her black skirt as she stepped out of the Fiat 124 Spider convertible Lucas owned, the wind teasing the fabric just enough to remind her it was shorter than she normally wore.

She hadn't noticed when she picked it—just grabbed the first thing that felt clean and forgettable. But now, with the night air licking her thighs and Lucas's hand on the small of her back, she suddenly felt exposed.

They were going to a steakhouse—his idea. Casual, familiar. Nothing flashy.

"You've been quiet," Lucas said as they crossed the parking lot.

"Long week," she replied. Longer month.

He smiled and gave her waist a gentle squeeze. The touch didn't hurt—not physically—but it made her skin crawl in a way it hadn't before. A year ago, that touch would've been comforting.

Now it felt… performative.

As they reached the entrance, something caught her attention. A weight. A pressure.

She turned her head—and froze. Two cars down. Black SUV. Tinted windows. Idle. No one else would've noticed. But she did. The famous KE, the Kingsman insignia, was prominently displayed on the rims. The unique shine of black chrome caught her attention. She knew that car, just like she knew his scent.

Her heart skipped.

Is he following me?

She turned back quickly, swallowing the lump in her throat. Lucas held the door open for her, and she nodded stiffly, stepping inside.

The hostess led them to the open-air balcony, and of course—because the universe had a twisted sense of humor—they were seated right at the edge.

This meant that the SUV remained visible. Parked. Waiting. She sat straighter. Crossed her legs. Fixed the hem of her skirt.

She hated how aware she became of her body under Alphonse's gaze—even when she couldn't see him. He was watching. She could feel it as surely as if his hand were on her thigh right now.

What are you doing, Alphonse?

Lucas said something about the menu, but she barely registered it. Her phone buzzed in her lap.

Alphonse [8:12PM]:
Wearing my skirt for him, sweetheart?

Her pulse quickened. She glanced at Lucas—still engrossed in the wine list—then typed quickly:

Freya [8:13PM]:
It's not your skirt.

Alphonse [8:14PM]:
It wraps around your hips like it remembers me.
Tell me… Is he getting a better view than I used to?

She swallowed hard. The memory of his hands on her, the press of his mouth against her neck, the way he spoke with his body—possessive, commanding—slipped into her thoughts like smoke through a crack.

Freya [8:15PM]:
You're insane.

The reply came faster this time.

Alphonse [8:15PM]:
Maybe.
But you haven't blocked me.
Which one of us is more dangerous?

She bit her lip, turned slightly away from Lucas, and typed with trembling fingers.

Freya [8:16PM]:
Stop. You're playing games.

And then—

Alphonse [8:16PM]:
You're playing with fire, Miss Blackwood.
Are you ready to burn?

Her legs clenched instinctively under the table. Her breath came shallow. She hated that she was reacting. Hated that he knew.

"Freya?" Lucas blinked. "Did you want to split a bottle or—?"

"Yeah. Sure. Red's fine," she said, voice tight.

He turned back to the menu, and her phone vibrated once more.

Alphonse [8:16PM]:
Enjoy your dinner, darling. I'll enjoy the view.
And when you get tired of pretending—

Another ping.

Alphonse [8:16PM]:
You know where I am.

She wanted to laugh. She wanted to turn around, march to that SUV, and kiss him until she forgot what it meant to be anyone else's. But for now, she took a sip of wine and forced a smile at Lucas.

Another ping.

"Someone's desperate," Lucas said, glancing at her phone.

Freya laughed lightly. "It's just work."

"Aren't you off today?" Lucas asked.

"Yes, but they're verifying some data. As the senior analyst on the case, it's my job to respond," she lied smoothly.

Alphonse [8:18PM]:
After all, I did promise I'd make you forget him by screaming my name as you come.

Her fingers hovered over the screen. The safe thing would be to say nothing. But Freya Blackwood had never been the safe thing.

She typed slowly.

Deliberately.
Each word a match struck in the dark.

Freya [8:19PM]:
You talk like you're the fire.
But maybe I'm the match, Kingsman.
And you're the one about to go up in flames.

She hit send. Then slid the phone face down on the table. And across the city, in the black SUV cloaked in shadows, she knew—he was smiling.

***

The moment the message appeared, Alphonse's eyes locked on the screen, the glow of her name slicing through the dark interior of the SUV.

Freya [8:19PM]:
You talk like you're the fire.
But maybe I'm the match, Kingsman.
And you're the one about to go up in flames.

A beat of silence. Then a slow, dangerous grin curled across his lips. She wasn't backing down. She never did.

His driver remained quiet, trained not to speak unless ordered, but Alphonse didn't notice him anyway. He was staring at the message like it had teeth. Like it bit him.

He leaned back, letting the tension in his jaw stretch into something else. Something heavier. Hotter.

"That's how you want to play it, sweetheart?" He murmured, his voice low enough to stay between him and the shadows.

She was the first woman to ever come at him like this— not chasing, not running, just… daring him. It was maddening. Addictive.

Because in her defiance, she wasn't saying no.
She was saying, Try me.

And Kingsmans didn't retreat from a challenge.

They consumed it.

Let her keep pretending she's still with that idiot.

Let her test the heat.

He adjusted the cuffs of his shirt with meticulous calm, eyes still on her contact name. Her words replayed over and over in his head, every syllable fanning the ache in his gut into something darker.

He wouldn't text back.

No.

That would be too straightforward.

Let her finish her cheap little dinner with Lucas. Let her feel bold and smug, sitting there with her wine and that skirt he wanted to rip off with his teeth.

The next time he touched her, it would not be from afar.

It wasn't going to be restrained.

She thought she was the match?

Then he'd show her what it meant to be caught in a Kingsman fire.

"Drive."

CHAPTER NINETEEN

Freya sat on the couch, her legs tucked beneath her as she swirled the wine in her glass, her mind spinning with the conversation. Across from her, Sofia watched her intently, arms folded, a skeptical look etched on her face.

"So… Lucas is getting better," Freya said, trying to sound casual, but even to her, the words felt hollow.

Sofia raised an eyebrow, clearly unconvinced. "Better how, exactly?" she asked, her voice tinged with doubt.

Freya hesitated, shrugging slightly as she tried to find the right words. "I don't know, he's just… trying more, you know? He's been different lately, more attentive. He's making an effort."

Sofia wasn't convinced. "Are you two having sex?" she asked bluntly, cutting straight to the point.

Freya's face flushed slightly, and she looked away, avoiding Sofia's gaze. "No."

"Then it's not okay, Freya," Sofia said, her tone firm.

Freya frowned, frustrated. "We don't need sex to make things work," she said, almost defensively. "There's more to a relatlonship than just that. We're working on other things— communication, trust."

Sofia shook her head, refusing to absolve her. "Sex is part of a relationship, Freya. It's where you create bonds. It's an intimate interaction that shows how much you care, how connected you are." Her voice softened slightly as she leaned forward. "You can't just ignore that part and pretend everything's fine. Without it, it's like there's this wall between you two."

Freya set her glass down, her fingers gripping the stem tightly. "I don't need that," she said quietly, her words more for herself than for Sofia. "It's not what defines our relationship."

Sofia sighed, her eyes narrowing slightly as she studied her friend. "What about Alphonse?"

Freya's breath caught at the mention of his name, her stomach tightening involuntarily. She glanced at Sofia, startled. "What about him?"

Sofia's eyes softened with understanding. "You didn't have to think about it with him, did you?" Her voice was gentle but pointed. "With Alphonse, the attraction was instant. It was natural. The connection was there without you having to force it."

Freya bit her lip, her thoughts racing. Sofia wasn't wrong, but she would rather not admit it. The truth was, her relationship with Lucas felt like something she was desperately trying to salvage, patching up pieces that had been broken for too long. But with Alphonse? It had been raw, unfiltered desire—something she couldn't ignore, no matter how much she wanted to.

Sofia leaned back, her eyes never leaving Freya's. "You can't hide from this forever, Freya. You deserve more than just 'better.' You deserve real connection. Whether it's with Lucas or someone else—hell, even Alphonse—you need to figure out what you want, what makes you happy."

Freya sat in silence, her thoughts swirling. She knew Sofia was right, but facing the reality of it scared her more than she wanted to admit.

"Alphonse is a strong character," Freya said, her voice low as she stared into her wine glass. "But he feels… unstable. One day he's as silent as death, and the next, he wants to fuck me in Lucas's bed."

Sofia's eyes widened, her hand flying to her mouth as she gasped. "Did he?" she asked, her voice a mix of shock and disbelief.

Freya's face flushed, the heat of the memory rising to the surface. She hesitated for a second before nodding, barely able to meet Sofia's eyes. "Yes."

The room went utterly still, the weight of Freya's confession hanging between them like a thick fog. Sofia blinked, taking in the full gravity of what her friend had just revealed. "Freya… what the hell?" she whispered, her voice laced with shock. "In Lucas's bed?"

Freya's pulse quickened as the moment replayed in her mind, her chest tightening. "Lucas was right outside the door," she admitted, her voice low and trembling. "And he didn't stop."

Sofia's eyes widened, her jaw dropping as she leaned forward, fully engrossed now. "How the fuck did you get away with that?"

Freya felt the tension building inside her, a tumultuous mix of shame and defiance churning in her gut. "I didn't plan for it, Sofia. It wasn't supposed to happen like that. He simply possesses the ability to deeply penetrate my emotions and elicit a response from me." She paused, struggling to find the right words. "When Alphonse is in the room, it's like I lose all control. He makes me forget… everything."

Sofia leaned forward, her expression somewhere between concern and fascination. "And you let him?"

Freya swallowed, her mind racing with conflicting emotions. "I didn't stop him," she admitted quietly, the shame creeping into her voice. "And I didn't want to." Her voice softened further, as if acknowledging the truth to Sofia made it feel all too real. "I wanted it, Sofia. Even though I knew it was wrong, even though I shouldn't have, I still wanted it."

Sofia was quiet for a moment, letting Freya's words settle in. Then, with a careful, measured tone, she asked, "Does Lucas know?"

Freya shook her head slowly, her fingers tightening around the edge of her glass. "No," she whispered. "Lucas doesn't know. And I can't ever tell him."

Sofia exhaled sharply, rubbing her forehead in disbelief. "Freya, this is… this is wild. You're putting yourself in danger. What are you going to do if Lucas finds out? I mean—Alphonse, in his bed? With Lucas outside the door? "

Freya leaned back on the couch, staring at the ceiling as a mixture of shame and excitement swirled in her chest. "I don't know, Sofia. It was like… the moment Alphonse was in the room, nothing else mattered. I couldn't think; I couldn't stop him. Hell, I didn't want to stop him." Her voice dropped, laced with frustration. "It's like I'm two different people with them. With Lucas, I feel this obligation, this weight of trying to make things work. But with Alphonse? He makes me feel… alive."

Sofia crossed her arms, her face a mix of concern and intrigue. "I get that, but Freya, you have to know this is going to blow up. Lucas might not know now, but eventually, he'll figure it out. Alphonse doesn't appear to be someone who should remain hidden."

Freya sighed, the weight of Sofia's words pressing down on her. She knew her friend was right—this situation couldn't last forever. But what choice did she have? Lucas had been striving to repair the damage, but the spark had vanished. And Alphonse? He was dangerous, thrilling, and everything she wasn't supposed to want but craved anyway.

Sofia watched her, her expression softening. "Freya, I know it feels exciting right now, but you can't live in this bubble. You've got to figure out what you really want—what's going to make you happy in the long run. Lucas? Alphonse? You can't keep them both."

Freya's chest tightened. She didn't know what she wanted. Or maybe she did, but admitting it felt too terrifying. "I know, Sofia," she whispered, her voice barely audible. "I just… I don't know how to let go of either of them."

Sofia reached out and squeezed Freya's hand gently, her voice soft but firm. "Whatever you decide, just make sure it's what you want. Not what you think you should do."

Before Freya could respond, her phone rang, and Layla's name flashed on the screen. Freya sighed, shaking her head. "The lost child appears."

"I know, I know, I'm late!" Layla's voice complained from the other end of the line. "I got caught up at work. What did I miss?"

Sofia remained unfazed. "Oh, nothing much. Just Freya having sex with Alphonse… in Lucas's bed… with Lucas outside the door."

Layla's scream pierced through the speaker. "What the fuck! Is this the same Freya I know!? That is savage! Does Alphonse have a brother? A cousin? A familiar? I feel like I'm missing out!"

Freya groaned, covering her face with her hands. "I didn't ask for it!"

"But you sure didn't stop him either!" Layla teased; her tone was carefree and teasing, as usual. "You're getting Triple-A treatment, girl! I mean, I know it's difficult to say no to that!"

Freya sighed, the weight of the situation still pressing heavily on her. "I'm still dealing with Lucas, though. I don't know how to—"

"Look, Freya," Layla interrupted, her voice suddenly more serious. "You might've spent years nourishing that relationship, but Lucas definitely wasn't doing the same the moment he went out looking for sex. If he had a problem, he should've spoken up. Did he? Did he ever say anything before he cheated?"

Freya went silent, the question hanging heavily between them.

"And that," Layla continued, her voice hardening, "shows the lack of dedication on his part. He didn't step up for both of you, and now, guess what? You found out there are better options out there. There are better men who know how to please you. Lucas isn't the only one, Freya! If a man is incapable of pleasing me or being honest with me, he lacks the courage to love me."

Freya sat there, speechless for a moment. Sofia nodded slowly, clearly agreeing with Layla.

Layla's voice came through again, lighter now. "Look, Freya, I know it's not easy. But you need to consider your needs and desires. What you want, what you need. Don't let Lucas guilt you into staying in something that doesn't make you happy."

Freya bit her lip, her mind racing. It was the truth she didn't want to face.

Layla's voice piped in one last time. "But hey, in the meantime, please let me know if Kingsman's got a cousin. I'm all for getting some of that billionaire action." She laughed, and Sofia rolled her eyes with a grin.

Freya couldn't help but let out a small laugh, feeling the weight on her chest lift just a little. Leave it to Layla to mix humour into the middle of a serious conversation. She appreciated it, though—it kept things from feeling too overwhelming.

Freya chuckled, shaking her head. "You're impossible, Layla."

"And you love me for it," Layla shot back.

***

The next meeting was scheduled beneath the Lexington Hotel—one of the many real estate acquisitions Freya had reviewed in the enterprise's records. Kingsman Enterprises had acquired the property not long ago. According to the files, the previous owner had been looking to retire, and the enterprise offered a deal too generous to refuse. Now, the Lexington served as a frequent site for internal seminars, high-end client events, and private meetings.

In fact, it was here—just beyond the polished marble lobby—that Freya had first met Alphonse's lawyer.

She expected today's meeting to be in one of the usual conference rooms near the lobby. But as she approached the corridor leading to them, a hotel employee stepped forward to intercept her.

"Excuse me, Miss Blackwood?"

She turned, surprised to be addressed.

The speaker was a young man, no more than nineteen. He wore the Lexington's signature wine-colored uniform trimmed in gold, though the suit looked a size too large for his thin frame. His nervous brown eyes flicked from her face to the floor as he extended a card toward her with both hands.

It was black, edged in gold, and embossed with the sleek KE logo—Kingsman Enterprises.

He bowed slightly, his voice soft and uncertain. "Mr. Kingsman is waiting for you in the VIP lounge on the 22nd floor."

Freya accepted the card with a polite nod, and the boy exhaled—relief evident in the slight, trembling smile that spread across his face. The braces on his teeth flashed as he smiled.

Had Alphonse terrified this poor kid into submission?

Before she could ask, he pointed toward the elevators, his hand still a little shaky. "You can take that one. It goes directly to the VIP suites."

Freya reached for her bag, instinctively prepared to tip him, but the boy quickly waved her off, shaking his head.

"Mr. Kingsman already took care of it," he said, almost reverently, then stepped back and gestured again to the elevator.

Freya hesitated for a moment, then slipped the card into her bag and made her way to the lift—uneasy now, not just from the sudden change in plans, but from the way the hotel itself seemed to bend in quiet reverence around one man's name.

Kingsman didn't just own the building. He *was* the building.

The elevator chimed softly as it reached the 22nd floor, the doors sliding open to reveal a private corridor bathed in muted gold lighting. Freya stepped out, her heels clicking lightly against the polished marble floor. The card the boy gave her fit perfectly into the door's scanner, which unlocked with a quiet hiss.

What greeted her on the other side stole her breath.

The suite was massive—designed like a secret haven carved into the sky. The polished slate floors felt cool to the touch, while the soft ivory tones of the walls reflected the morning sun filtering in through the massive glass windows. Ahead of her, a rectangular indoor pool gleamed like liquid sapphire in the center of the space, steam rising gently from its surface. Sleek, dark stone tiles surrounded the pool, with modern lounging couches arranged tastefully around it, a few towels draped neatly over their backs.

To her left was a curved staircase with glass railing that spiraled upward—likely leading to the sleeping quarters. A small but fully stocked bar stood in the corner, its mirrored shelves catching glints of sunlight and casting them onto the floor in soft, dancing patterns.

The suite was breathtaking, elegant in a way that whispered of opulence without ever needing to shout it. It was the kind of place Layla would throw a party in—a wild, champagne-drenched night with music echoing off the high ceilings. But despite the quiet, the suite felt like it held secrets. It seemed as though it had witnessed a great deal. Heard things. It felt as if it had recollected past events.

Freya set her bag down on one of the low charcoal couches and walked toward the pool, the light making ripples dance across the ceiling. That was when she saw it—a figure at the bottom.

Motionless.

Her heart lurched.

"Alphonse?" she called out, voice tightening.

No answer. The water shimmered above him, softening the edges of his form like a dream. He lay suspended just above the bottom, black boxer briefs clinging to him like a second skin. His body was statuesque—tattoos sprawled across his chest and arms, muscular and lean like a man sculpted by pressure. His inked skin moved only with the water. His hair, usually slicked back, floated around his temples like a dark halo.

Panic surged through her like electricity.

Freya kicked her heels off in one breathless motion and dove in.

The shock of the cold water hit her skin as she cut through it, bubbles spiraling around her. She swam closer, the current she created brushing against him. Her hand reached out, fingers grazing the firm plane of his chest.

Then his eyes opened.

Icy blue.

His eyes were as clear as ever.

She gasped, startled—an air bubble escaping her mouth, thinning her oxygen too fast. Her body jolted back instinctively, heart hammering.

In an instant, his arms were around her, powerful and fluid, pulling her up and out of the water like she weighed nothing.

They broke the surface with a sharp splash. Freya gasped for air, coughing once, her hands clutching his shoulders.

"Jesus," she breathed.

His lips were close—his breath calm despite the chaos in hers. "I thought you were smarter than that," Alphonse murmured, his voice rough from disuse but tinged with warmth. "You didn't think I was dead, did you?"

She glared up at him, chest heaving. "You weren't moving."

"I was thinking."

"In a pool?"

His smirk deepened. "Best place to drown the noise."

Her hands stayed on him, reluctant to let go.

"You scared me," she whispered, her voice barely rising above the lapping water.

Alphonse's gaze held hers, unwavering. "Do you jump into pools for every man who scares you?"

Freya let out a shaky laugh, brushing wet hair from her face. "Only the ones who confuse the hell out of me."

He smirked, the corners of his mouth tilting with that infuriating, magnetic confidence. "Good. I'd hate to think I'm not special."

She rolled her eyes, but her heart fluttered with excitement. "You're impossible."

"I prefer... singular," he replied smoothly.

He shifted her gently to the edge of the pool and lifted himself out with ease, water cascading down his sculpted frame. The muscles of his back flexed with every movement, tattoos glistening under the golden morning light.

He remained completely and shamelessly delicious.

Freya's mouth dried up, her heart quivering as he strode across the tiles as if he possessed every inch of space in the suite.

Of course, he did.

Without turning, he grabbed a large, plush towel off the back of one of the chairs, then turned and extended it toward her, his expression unreadable but his gaze dark with amusement.

"Are you going to keep staring, or are you going to dry off before I make you drip all over my floors?"

She climbed out, water trickling down her skin, and snatched the towel from his hand. "You've got a pool in your living room. I think you can survive a few puddles."

"Correction," he said, already walking away, voice echoing through the quiet space, "I have a pool in one of my hotel rooms."

Freya laughed under her breath as she wrapped the towel around herself. "Right. Silly me. How many rooms are there in this place again?"

He didn't answer.

She followed the sound of ice clinking behind the bar and found him pouring a drink—still very, very wet—his back to her, posture relaxed like this was just any other morning.

She stood there, half-drenched, staring at a man who embodied pure temptation.

"I feel like I'm in a Bond movie," she muttered, pulling the towel tighter around her. "Except Bond usually has pants."

Alphonse turned his head slightly, a slow grin spreading across his lips. "That's where Bond and I part ways."

He slid a glass across the bar to her, amber liquid catching the morning light. "You dive into my pool uninvited, and I reward you with 30-year scotch. Try doing that in MI6."

Freya took the glass, shaking her head. "This is the weirdest breakfast I've ever had."

Alphonse leaned in across the bar, his voice lowering. "Then let me ruin every breakfast after."

She held his gaze, heart thudding, lips parted. His dark hair dripped water down the sharp lines of his face, and gods— heat was already pooling low in her body, coiling dangerously.

He set the empty glass on the bar and closed the distance between them. His hand reached for her shoulder, sweeping the damp strands of her hair behind it. Then his fingers drifted down the slope of her neck, brushing the edge of the towel, easing it aside as his eyes traced the outline of her damp clothes.

"You should get out of those clothes before you catch a cold," he murmured.

Freya arched a brow. "Is this your idea of getting me naked?"

His grin was sin itself. "Whether you jumped in the pool or not, Miss Blackwood, I would've gotten there eventually. You just made it justifiable."

She let out a sharp breath—part irritation, part amusement. Of course, she'd walked right into one of Alphonse's games. With a huff, she grabbed the towel and flung it in his face.

He caught it with one hand, grinning, thoroughly unbothered.

She turned on her heel—but the sleek tile floor betrayed her. Her feet slipped out from under her, and a startled gasp escaped her lips.

Two strong arms caught her mid-fall, locking her tightly against a bare chest.

Her breath caught—not from the slip, but from the unmistakable, rigid press against her lower back.

Alphonse's voice came low, amused, and dark. "Now who's making things justifiable?"

Freya didn't move, pulse roaring in her ears. His hands flexed against her waist, fingers splayed like he was memorizing every curve. The heat between them cracked like lightning, silent but overwhelming.

He leaned in, lips grazing the shell of her ear. "Careful," he whispered. "Keep falling like that, and I might never let you get up."

His grip didn't loosen. If anything, it tightened.

Alphonse held her flush against him, one hand sliding from her waist up to her ribs—slow, deliberate. He knew what he was doing. Every touch was precise. Calculated. Dangerous.

"Still want to play games, Miss Blackwood?" He murmured against her neck, his breath warm and teasing against her damp skin.

Freya's lips parted, but no sound came out. Her heart pounded, her body betraying her completely—melting back into him like she belonged there. Her legs were no longer her own. They trembled slightly beneath her, useless against the gravity of him.

His mouth brushed the corner of her jaw and she felt it everywhere.

"I warned you," he said, his voice like velvet soaked in sin. "You stepped into this willingly."

She didn't speak. Couldn't.

As soon as his palm slid flat over her stomach and down, brushing the waistband of her drenched clothes, Freya swore the air left the room.

His fingers teased her skin with excruciating restraint as he said, "Say it." "This is what you want."

She leaned her head back on his shoulder. He unraveled her so easily, and she hated it. She hated the way the truth made her lips quiver.

"Yes," she whispered. "I want this."

That was all he needed.

In one fluid movement, he turned her in his arms, lifting her effortlessly and carrying her the few steps to the lounge sofa tucked near the window, its cushions dark and luxurious. He sat down, pulling her astride him, her knees bracketing his thighs.

"You're not wearing these clothes anymore," he said, gripping the hem of her shirt. "Lift your arms."

His eyes darkened as the soaked fabric peeled away, revealing damp skin and flushed curves. He traced his thumbs up her sides, watching her reactions like a man starving.

"You don't get to hide from me," he murmured, nibbling along her collarbone, down between her breasts. "In flimsy dinner night."

She gasped when his hands gripped her hips, grinding her against the intense length of him, with only the thin layers of damp fabric separating their heat.

Freya bit her lip, her fingers digging into his shoulders. "Alphonse…"

His eyes met hers—feral, possessive, electric.

"You're mine."

Then he took her mouth—slow and deep—his tongue firestroking against hers like he owned the rhythm of her heartbeat. She moaned into him, arching, aching, chasing more. Her body was no longer her own. It moved at his pace, to his touch, as if he'd written her skin into his script long ago.

Freya's breath hitched. Heat surged through her, pooling low in her belly. Her eyes searched his, finding no trace of hesitation—only raw desire wrapped in lethal control.

His hands moved beneath the hem of her soaked skirt, fingers brushing the bare skin of her thighs, slow and maddening, drawing shivers out of her with every touch. With exquisite control, he peeled her damp skirt down her thighs, inch by inch, watching every reaction ripple through her. His fingers brushed the inside of her thighs again—only this time, the touch was deliberate. Intimate.

"Look at you," he murmured, trailing a single finger along her thighs, just enough to tease without giving. "Already trembling. I haven't even started."

She clenched her fingers into his shoulders, trying to ground herself, but the feel of him—bare skin under her palms, the taut muscle beneath—only made her want more. Then he peeled her damp underwear down her thighs, letting it fall atop the skirt.

His mouth curved slightly, predatory. "Tell me what you want, Freya."

She hesitated, lips parted, cheeks flushed—her body betraying every shred of composure.

"I want to feel you," she whispered, her breath barely audible over the thrum of her heartbeat.

Alphonse's grip on her tightened. "Wrong answer," he growled low, the sound curling around her spine like smoke. "Try again. Tell me what you want from me."

His hand traced along the curve of her lower back, fingers dipping just beneath the curves of her ass. Freya shivered, her forehead resting against his. The scent of him was dizzying.

It was maddening, the way her body responded to him. It felt as though her body was already familiar with his touch. This rhythm. This danger. Lucas had kissed her with practiced charm; Alphonse touched her like a man who knew how to ruin and remake.

And right now, ruin never looked more inviting.

She let her breath catch, letting the heat pooling in her belly guide her.

"I want you to take me," she murmured. "Like it's the last thing you'll ever do."

His stillness was sharper than motion—like a predator just before the strike.

Then his mouth was on hers again—hot, demanding, a claim rather than a kiss. His hands swept her up like she weighed nothing, and when he pulled back, his voice scraped against her lips, deep and dark.

"Now that's better."

She barely registered the way he sat, pulling her into his lap, until his eyes locked with hers again.

"Show me," he said. His command was both soft and devastating. "How much you need me."

He leaned back into the lounge sofa, his eyes never leaving her as the corners of his lips curved into a smirk. She pulled off Alphonse's underwear with a swift motion. He lifted his hips effortlessly to assist her in slipping the underwear off of him. His hard erection was now fully exposed.

She positioned herself, knees between his hips, and leveled down. Her body tightened, and a soft moan escaped her, accompanied by a satisfying grunt. As she started to move, she tried to keep her eyes open to see a reaction from Alphonse, but the feeling was overwhelming. She found herself closing her eyes and giving in to the sensation.

The sound of wet slapping skin filled the room as her body moved and rocked, enjoying the feeling his body provided. Alphonse pulled her down harder, his movements mirroring her rhythm. "Fuck," he breathed out. "Fucking good."

With a twist of his hip, he pulled her down onto the sofa, rolling onto her body. He was now on top of her, his hands spreading her thighs wide. He slammed into her, his movements fierce and relentless, hitting her G-spot.

"Oh God," she huffed.

"Say it," he breathed out, moving faster. "What do you want?"

She gasped, her body trembling with pleasure. "I want to come!" she rasped out, her voice barely audible over the sound of their bodies crashing together. Alphonse's movements became even more frantic, his body driving into hers with a primal intensity.

Those words that break them into the instinct of an animal. They were compelled to assert their dominance, to come forward, and to fulfill their part. It's a powerful word that drives them into sultry motivation.

This six-foot, muscular, cold, handsome man looked even more desirable, seducing her with all his strength as if there were no tomorrow. It was the peak of a perfect flooding release.

"It's so good!" she moaned, her body trembling on the edge of orgasm. Alphonse groaned, his body tensing as he felt her muscles clenching around him. He was close, so close to his release.

She felt him throb inside her, his body shuddering with the force of his orgasm. "Oh god, Alphonse," she moaned, her body trembling with pleasure. Alphonse collapsed back down to the couch, his body trembling with the aftershocks of his release.

He was still inside her, his erection throbbing with the aftershocks of his orgasm. She wrapped her arms around him, holding him close as he trembled with pleasure. She could feel his heart pounding in his chest, his body still pulsing with the aftershocks of their intimacy.

His body was damp with sweat, hair clinging to his forehead, and those icy eyes locked onto hers with a satisfied, primal hunger that made Freya tremble all over again.

However, a sharp and jarring sound from his phone interrupted the moment abruptly, echoing across the quiet room.

Alphonse's jaw tightened. With a guttural growl, he pulled back, slipping out of her warmth. The sudden absence was startling.

He snatched the phone from the nearby table. "This better be—"

He stopped mid-sentence. His expression shifted in an instant—rage melting into something colder, sharper.

"I'll be there in ten," he said flatly, his voice suddenly all business. Then he hung up.

Freya sat up slowly. "Is everything okay?"

Alphonse was already stepping into his pants. He moved with quiet precision, reaching for his shirt. From his discarded jacket, he pulled out a sleek black card, trimmed in gold.

"Use this," he said, handing it to her without meeting her eyes. "Call for a change of clothes. Anything you need—room service will handle it."

She stared at the card, then back at him, confused. "You're leaving?"

"I'll be out of town for the week," he said, slipping into his shoes, then buttoning the shirt without a glance. "I'll contact you when I return."

"Wait—Alphonse—"

But he was already at the door, fingers sliding through his damp hair, face unreadable once again.

And then he was gone, leaving behind the scent of cologne, the echo of his touch, and a quiet, empty room that no longer felt quite so warm.

Freya stood in the echoing silence of the suite, wrapped in the towel, her skin cooling where Alphonse's heat had been.

Why did he leave so suddenly?

She reached for her phone and her bag, intending to distract herself—when a breaking news alert lit up the screen.

Kingsman Enterprises Faces Major Setback: Multi-Million Dollar Project Stalls Due to Mismanagement

Her breath caught.

She tapped the article. The words blurred as her eyes scanned through the details. A web of delays and financial complications now ensnared one of Alphonse's most ambitious developments—a high-profile, internationally backed project. A mismanaged team under his command bore the blame. Headlines hinted at public fallout. Investor unrest.

It was a PR disaster.

And in that moment, everything clicked.

The shadows she'd noticed under his eyes, the tension in his shoulders, the way his phone had been buzzing even when he was with her. This wasn't about avoiding her. It wasn't even about control.

Alphonse had a kingdom to protect. And kings didn't rest when the walls were cracking.

Still, the understanding did little to ease the hollow ache spreading in her chest. He had left. Abruptly. Without explanation. He left without even glancing back.

Freya stepped toward the window, resting a hand against the glass. The city sprawled beneath her—cold, vast, unreachable. Her reflection stared back, half-shadowed in the glass. And in that quiet, she saw it clearly:

She wasn't just frustrated. She wasn't just curious.

She was in deeper than she'd ever intended to fall.

And that realization brought a cold rush of fear. She realized that her love for Alphonse Kingsman was not secure. It wasn't steady. She stood on the brink of something immense, aware that it had the potential to consume her completely.

She didn't know if he'd return to pick up where they left off.

Or perhaps this—whatever it was—had already started to unravel.

But one thing was painfully clear.

This was no longer a game.

And she wasn't sure if she was ready to win or lose it.

***

The office was quiet. Too quiet.

Only the soft hum of the city beyond the glass wall remained, muffled by double-glazed windows and the weight of too many secrets.

Alphonse sat behind his desk, a cigarette smoldering between two fingers, the smoke curling lazily in front of his face as his eyes scanned the open folder before him.

At the center of the file sat a photograph—a mugshot.

The man in it wore a smug, too-practiced smile. Tan skin, bleached teeth, and a gold chain barely hidden beneath the collar of a silk shirt. He was the type of man who earned his livelihood by persuading women that they were the only ones present in the room.

Freddy Morales.

He worked as a hotel project manager.

He was a smooth-talking opportunist who had slipped through too many cracks—until now.

Beside the folder, lying quiet but not forgotten, was a matte black Glock 19. Its surface reflected nothing, but it made a statement all its own.

Alphonse took one last drag of his cigarette, snuffed it out with a swift flick, then reached for the pistol. He checked the chamber, loaded it with practiced ease, and slid it into the holster beneath his suit jacket with a cold efficiency that belonged to another world.

One, he didn't show Freya.

The door opened behind him with a soft knock. Lydia stepped in, heels clicking against the floor, a manila envelope in one hand, and a set of keys in the other. She didn't flinch when her eyes fell on the gun. She never did.

"Car's waiting. And Charlie confirmed the location," she said, offering both items.

Alphonse stood, buttoning his coat as he took the folder from the desk and handed it to her.

"That bad?" he asked.

Lydia nodded once. "Worse. We have evidence, but word is he's been running a side operation. Girls. Drugs. Clients. Under your name."

His jaw tightened. He didn't speak. He didn't need to.

"Tell Charlie I'll be there."

Lydia gave a small nod, turned, and disappeared without another word.

Alphonse stood still for a moment, staring at the mugshot one last time before snapping the folder shut. His eyes flicked to his phone, glowing silently on the desk.

Freya's name lit the top of the screen.

He bit the inside of his cheek. He hated how he'd left her at the hotel—naked, confused, with no answers. But the task required every ounce of him. Distraction wasn't a luxury. Not in this world.

He picked up the phone and scrolled through his contacts until he landed on the one he needed. He pressed call.

"Get your ass off whatever dick you're on. I want you in my office. Wednesday."

There was a burst of laughter coming from the other end. "Jesus. Hello to you too, cousin."

He hung up. Pocketing the phone, Alphonse turned toward the door.

Gone was the CEO. The strategist. He was a man who wore five-thousand-dollar suits and discussed luxury real estate over champagne.

What walked out that office now...

It was something colder.

He grew up in the shadows of an empire that was not built but rather seized.

Not Alphonse Kingsman.

Alphonse Kingsman was the inheritor of a much darker legacy.

And someone was about to remember why you never cross a **Kingsman**.

ACKNOWLEDGEMENT

Kingsman was never meant to follow rules. It wasn't outlined or tamed—it was written on instinct, emotion, and late-night bursts of "screw it, let's go." Unlike Under the Sky and DFurious, which followed the outlines and arcs of controlled emotions, Kingsman came to life in motion—I wrote it as I ran, without boundaries, and with fire in my chest.

To my supporters on Inkitt—thank you. You reviewed my work, provided insightful feedback, and encouraged my progress during times when the chaos within my mind rendered my thoughts incomprehensible on paper. You made me feel like this story mattered, and that's something I'll never take for granted.

To my husband—thank you for sitting beside me night after night, watching Tulsa King, throwing in wild ideas, and matching my energy when inspiration struck at the most inconvenient hours. This story wouldn't exist without your steady presence and your genuine curiosity for this crazy world I built. I wrote this one in its raw form. Written fast. I wrote it as if I had a point to prove—to no one but myself. Thank you for taking this ride with me. We're just getting started.

ABOUT THE AUTHOR

Liliz Black, is a passionate storyteller from San Juan, Puerto Rico. Her love for reading and writing was sparked by the *Harry Potter* series, which also played a key role in helping her learn English. Bilingual in Spanish and English, she grew up imagining bold "what if" scenarios that later bloomed into full-fledged stories.

She began her writing journey with fanfiction before branching into original works, where she now builds complex universes that span romance, fantasy, drama, and dark intrigue. Under the name **Liliz Black**, she writes bold, emotional stories for adult audiences, while keeping **Yaniliz Negrón** for her family-friendly and children's projects.

She studied graphic design and game design at Atlantic College and currently lives in San Juan with her husband, their two children, two dogs, and seven cats. Whether she's designing, writing, or caring for her pets, creativity is at the heart of everything she does.

Follow her journey and dive into her worlds:

- **Instagram:** @lilizblack
- **Facebook:** @LBLilizBlack

Check out More

Here's a preview for the first chapter of the next book:

The grand hotel near the coast loomed against the backdrop of the ocean, its sleek design blending modern elegance with a hint of timeless luxury. With its sleek design that blended modern elegance with a dash of traditional luxury, the grand hotel by the sea loomed over the ocean. Workers were dispersed along the scaffolding, painting and adding finishing touches to the mostly finished structure. The azure waves were reflected by the building's gleaming glass façade, and the distant cries of seagulls blended with the steady sound of hammers and drills.

A Bentley in black matte glided into the hotel lobby's broad, circular driveway. The shiny exterior of the car contrasted sharply with the dust and activity of the building site. A bald, imposing figure emerged from the building as the car came to a stop close to the entrance. His presence demanded notice. Despite his diminutive stature, his muscular physique and rugged features conveyed a no-nonsense authority. The man had the air of someone who had seen and done more than most, and he was dressed in a well-tailored gray suit that somehow managed to look both formal and intimidating.

Though his vitality suggested otherwise, he looked older than his years, with small wrinkles around his sharp hazel eyes. He raised an eyebrow, obviously intrigued, as his eyes fell upon the Bentley. Without hesitation, he walked toward the driver's side, his gait steady and deliberate, and knocked on the window with a rough, confident hand.

"Where's César?" he said in a gravelly, unrepentant New York accent.

Alphonse removed his sunglasses and slipped them into his suit pocket as the car door opened with a deliberate click. He was dressed in a black suit that was perfectly tailored, and after adjusting his handcuffs, he answered in a composed but authoritative tone. "César is occupied with other tasks that I gave him."

With a smirk tugging at the corner of his lips, the bald man held up his hands in a mock defensive gesture. "Well, it's weird not seeing you with your favorite bodyguard." His voice carried an edge of humor, but his eyes remained sharp, assessing.

Alphonse shot him a glare, the kind that could silence a room. As he shut the door behind him, his movements deliberate and precise, he straightened his lapels before speaking in a low, clipped tone. "What the fuck, Charlie?"

Charlie snorted, unbothered by the clear irritation in Alphonse's voice. "Shit hit the fan," he said bluntly. "I can only do so much in this legal shitshow you've got going on."

Alphonse's eyes narrowed as he regarded Charlie. Although Charlie was three inches shorter, he still had an imposing presence. The two locked eyes, and an unspoken understanding passed between them. With his typical irreverence, Charlie broke the moment with a groan. "The joke your Dickmans placed us in? It's a real piece of shit, Alpha. You know I'll dig through dirt, but even I ain't a Kingsman."

Alphonse's jaw tightened, his patience visibly thinning. With a calm and assured gait, he turned toward the hotel's entrance and ordered, "Details." Charlie trailed closely behind, his rough manner standing in stark contrast to Alphonse's refined grace.

Charlie went on as they entered the opulent lobby, which was still under construction but already gave off an air of grandeur with its high ceilings and shiny marble floors. "The real shit? They're pocketing money. Big time. But here's the kicker." He lowered his voice and glanced around to ensure that no one else could hear him. "Contacts are saying there's poppies and trafficking involved."

The words made Alphonse stop abruptly. His polished shoes clicked against the marble, the only sound in the sudden stillness. He turned abruptly, staring at Charlie with his piercing eyes. "Are you certain?" he asked, his voice cold and controlled, but a dangerous edge lurked beneath the calm.

Charlie placed a hand over his chest, his expression earnest. "Up to my heart, man," he said, thumping his fist against his chest for emphasis. "I don't like it any more than you do. After everything we've worked for, it's a fucking mess. But it's exactly what I called."

Alphonse's face darkened, his thoughts already racing as he processed the implications. The lines between business and criminal enterprise were always sharp in his dealings, and the idea of crossing into this level of corruption threatened to upend everything he had built. His fingers brushed against the cufflink on his wrist, a subtle grounding gesture, as he steadied himself.

"Do you have names?" he asked finally, his tone clipped.

Charlie nodded. "A few. This ain't surface-level shit. This is rotten to the core."

"But I do have the shit show here sitting," he added with a smirk. "I thought you could ask him yourself."

The dimly lit casino floor was eerily silent, the usual cacophony of whirring slot machines and shuffling cards conspicuously absent. The construction materials strewn about revealed the ongoing work, and the machines stood idle, their screens dark. The large room's unfinished atmosphere was further enhanced by the soft clink of tools and the faint hum of fluorescent lights.

The sound of Alphonse's polished shoes hitting the tiled floor echoed through the deserted casino as he walked in with a slow, steady step. As he led the way through the skeletal structure of what would soon be a playground for the elite, Charlie trailed closely behind him, his smirk never going away.

As he looked around, Charlie said in a casual tone, "It's still a bit of a ghost town." "But give it time. Once the lights come on, this place will be flooded with cash—and problems."

Alphonse didn't respond, his sharp eyes scanning the space. He absorbed every detail, noting the layout and imagining the flow of patrons that would eventually fill the space. His thoughts, however, weren't on the aesthetics; they were firmly fixed on the business at hand.

They walked over to a temporary arrangement in the far corner, where a comfortable table had been transformed into a space for spontaneous meetings. A man sat slouched in a chair, his ostentatious clothing standing out sharply against the minimalist surroundings. Freddy. His overly tight suit and flashy gold watch shouted desperation under the guise of confidence, but his shaky manner revealed the deception.

Freddy was flanked by two muscular men in leather jackets, their stances rigid and uncompromising. Freddy, already perspiring through his designer shirt, was unfazed by their piercing glares. When he saw Alphonse coming, his uneasiness turned into a full-blown panic attack.

"Mr. Kingsman!" Freddy blurted, scrambling to stand. His nerves were palpable, his voice strained as he tried—and failed—to project composure. "I wasn't expecting you so soon!"

The two guards beside Freddy didn't budge, and with a subtle gesture from Charlie, they shoved him back into his seat without ceremony.

Alphonse stopped a few feet away, his presence commanding the room without the need for words. He pulled out a chair across from Freddy and sat down with calculated precision. His movements were slow and deliberate, each one designed to unsettle the man before him.

Freddy's anxious gaze flicked to Charlie and back to Alphonse. With his hands wringing, he stumbled, "I—I can explain everything." "I can assure you that there has been a misunderstanding."

Alphonse's expression remained impassive, his gaze cold and unwavering. "Freddy," he said, his voice low and measured, "do you think I came all the way here for misunderstandings?"

Freddy's lips parted as if to reply, but no sound came out. He swallowed hard, his eyes flickering to the two guards still standing ominously at his sides.

Alphonse leaned forward slightly, resting his forearms on the table. "We should have completed the hotel weeks ago," he began, his tone calm but laced with a quiet menace. Yet here we are. Explain."

Freddy licked his lips nervously, his hands fidgeting in his lap. "There've been… delays," he said haltingly. "Decorations for the VIP suites have been costly, and, well, unforeseen expenses popped up. But it's all for the benefit of the project, I swear!"

Charlie snorted, crossing his arms as he leaned against a nearby pillar. "Freddy, you're digging yourself a hole. And trust me, Alphonse isn't the type to hand out shovels."

Alphonse didn't break his gaze, his silence cutting deeper than any words. There was an obvious sense of pressure in the room, and Freddy's anxious babble filled the silence.

"I didn't mean for things to spiral, Mr. Kingsman," Freddy continued, his voice cracking. "It's just—sometimes you have to grease a few palms to keep things running smoothly. Nothing major, just… routine stuff."

"Routine," Alphonse reiterated, his voice unwavering. No rage. No rise. A chilly calculation was all that was done. He didn't need to shout because power didn't yell. It applied pressure.

He shifted his gaze to the man beside Freddy—a silent command. The guard reacted instantly, grabbing Freddy by the back of the neck and slamming his face into the table.

CRACK.

The sound echoed through the abandoned casino floor like a warning shot fired in marble and dust.

Freddy let out a sharp, panicked cry, blood smearing across the polished wood as he clutched his face, nose clearly broken, breath ragged.

"P-please—I didn't—"

"Enough," Alphonse said. Quiet. Measured. The silence was so intense that it caused men to perspire profusely.

Even the guards froze, tension coiling in the room as Alphonse slowly drew his matte black Glock with a silencer attached, raised it, and pressed the barrel against Freddy's blood-slick forehead. Freddy whimpered, the cold steel making him visibly shake.

"Let's skip the excuses." Alphonse's voice dropped to a whisper. "Where did the money go?"

Freddy stammered, "I—I just moved some funds—temporary—I thought it'd boost profits—expand the project—this guy, Stall, he—he said it was a sure thing."

The Glock pressed harder. "Stall," Alphonse echoed darkly.

"Yeah—yeah—he said you'd be fine with it! He said you were already in talks with his associate. Said this was just—just good business—'Human trafficking is a goldmine,' he told me."

Freddy coughed up blood and desperation. "I—I thought you'd approve! The drug, called Nexis, is synthetic and volatile, but it sells for a very high price overseas. He said it'd double the hotel income under the table. You always emphasize the importance of thinking globally—having a bigger scope, right?

Alphonse's eyes didn't flinch. "Who's his associate?" he asked coldly.

Freddy blinked. "Whitemore."

The mention of that name resonated sharply, like a gunshot. Alphonse's jaw ticked. His grip tightened.

He pulled the Glock back a few inches—then drove it forward again, square against Freddy's forehead. His voice was calm. But lethal.

"There's one rule in my house, Freddy. We don't touch that shit. We do not engage in human trafficking. No Nexis. No stains that scream terrible news."

He held Freddy's terrified gaze for one last second. He then pulled the trigger.

www.ingramcontent.com/pod-product-compliance
Lightning Source LLC
Chambersburg PA
CBHW071117100726
47908CB00008B/2401